UNLOCKING FEAR

Keys to Love, Book One

Kennedy Layne

UNLOCKING FEAR

Dedication

Jeffrey—You hold the key to my heart.

Cole—Your future is bright with many doors to walk through...try them all and enjoy the journeys!

A captivating romantic suspense series from USA Today Bestselling Author Kennedy Layne where seduction burns but danger is never far behind...

A chance mishap with a sledgehammer was the sole reason a chilling nightmare was unleashed in Blyth Lake.

Noah Kendall's grisly discovery left him in the middle of a murder investigation and a neighbor who knew more than she was willing to say. Reese Woodward had returned to town with dark secrets, and he was determined to unravel them. While evil lurks in the darkness, seduction burns between them...only time was their enemy.

Will her secrets destroy what they've built, or can he earn her trust before the killer strikes again?

CHAPTER ONE

Twelve years ago…

THE DEEPENING SHADOWS stretched out across the small cluster of trees, causing the footpath to become somewhat obscured by the dark. The dying leaves that covered the floor of the woods rustled as the cool October breeze turned into a strong gust of wind.

A storm must be rolling into town.

Emma didn't slow down her pace. She was already an hour late for her curfew, but at least this old shortcut would take ten minutes off her trip home. Her parents would probably ground her for at least a week, if not more. She needed to find a better way to sneak back inside the house. The back door squeaked horribly. It could wake the dead.

What was the odd chance her sister would cover for her?

Emma grimaced, already knowing the answer to that question. This was all Shae's fault, anyway. Why did she always get the car, just because she was older? It was so unfair that she didn't have to share.

Emma quickened her pace despite the darkness and the chance of tripping over a root. She imagined that she could walk this route with her eyes closed just as easily. She'd come this way a thousand times over. It was used by most of the kids who were still relegated to riding their bikes and walking out to Yoder's farm to party, especially since most of them lived on the far side of the old woods in town.

A twig snapped in the distance, bringing her up short. Its piercing crack echoed off the trees. Was someone else walking home?

"Who's there?"

Emma waited for a reply, wincing when her voice was amplified through the small stretch of woods. She tried to peer through the trees, expecting to see Brynn or Julie, but it was too dark to make anything out beyond a few yards.

The faint and comforting sound of her favorite song drifted from the old farmhouse. She looked over her shoulder, still able to make out the orange sparks rising from the top of the raging bonfire as they reached into the night's sky. It was almost as if the flames were dancing, reminding her of how Billy held her in his arms earlier as they swayed to the music.

Emma smiled as she wrapped her arms around her waist in an effort to keep warm. She could still smell the bonfire on her sweater, along with his father's cologne that Billy had been wearing. Maybe he graduated to buying his own though, choosing from the limited selection at Murphy's dry goods. Not even the chilly night air could take away her happiness at having secured a chance at a relationship. She'd waited so long for him to notice her.

Tonight had been as perfect as it could get.

Now all she had to do was figure out a way to sneak into her house without her parents catching her in the act or that stupid door screeching out into the night. She needed to be able to say yes to Billy if he asked her out for next weekend. And he would, she was sure of it.

Emma slowly spun around looking for the source of the noise, not seeing anyone or anything. A quick glance up at the sky told her that the clouds were gathering. She hesitated before walking deeper into the woods that would lead her right to the edge of Seventh Street and the town's cemetery.

A vision of her standing by her school locker and saying yes to Billy had her continuing forward with a determined stride.

This annual bonfire wouldn't be their last, of that she was certain, but it was one she would always remember.

She'd heard that old Yoder's farm had been sold, so future get-togethers would most likely be in the clearing on the north side of the woods. She noticed the new owners had even started renovating the farmhouse, but that hadn't stopped Chad Schaeffer from organizing one last bash out by the farm pond. It was a miracle the sheriff hadn't cruised by earlier and sent everyone home. He was usually a real stickler when it came to parties involving the local teens.

No one recognized the name of the new owner. There were no relatives of the Yoders around these parts anymore, so the town council must have decided to auction off the land after clearing it with the courts. She'd meant to ask her dad how someone determined if a piece of property was derelict. She'd heard a teacher talking about it in class. It probably had something to do with property taxes.

Emma hadn't wanted to bring up the matter, because then her dad would have figured out that she was part of the gang who hung out on the same property the town council complained about.

Now that would have earned her a grounding for at least a month or more.

There was a break in the clouds, allowing for the dirt path in front of her to suddenly became clear. She took another step forward before realizing something was quite wrong, but by then it was far too late.

Emma walked directly into the arms of her killer.

CHAPTER TWO

Present day...

THE BLUE AND white aluminum sign declaring Blyth Lake had a population of two thousand, three hundred, and four citizens had seen better days. The anodized metal was faded from exposure to endless days of sunshine, not to mention the dents on the sides from all the beer cans that had been thrown at it. It didn't help that the once-white letters had blurred to the point of appearing almost unreadable.

None of that mattered, though.

The old town's welcome post signified home.

Noah Kendall resisted the urge to drive through the small town to see what had changed and what still remained the same as it had for his entire life. He'd been born and raised in Blyth Lake, second to the youngest of the five notorious Kendall children. There was something to be said about returning to one's roots, and the warm memories began to filter back one by one as he noted different landmarks.

Damn, it was good to be home.

He rolled the windows down on his late model black F150, allowing the warm summer air to fill the cab with a bouquet of familiar scents. The faint breeze brought with it the light fragrances of honeysuckle and lilacs. The two old oak trees on either side of the upcoming four-way stop had matured over the years, but the vibrant flowers and plants surrounding the thick trunks remained the same as they had always been.

It was clear to him that Ms. Barmore must still oversee the town's formal landscaping. She always did have a thing for honeysuckle and lilacs.

Noah pulled his truck to a stop at the first intersection and rested his fingers on the turn signal, giving it a second thought. The urge to drive straight ahead was there, but he did what was expected of him and flipped up the lever to indicate his left turn.

Family came first.

Family was everything.

His father, Gus Kendall, was without a doubt waiting for him at the family home.

This homecoming was bittersweet. It would be only the second time Noah returned to Blyth Lake that his mother, Mary Kendall, wouldn't be standing on the front porch with open arms. The first time Noah had returned to town without his mom greeting him had been three years ago for her funeral. It was then that his brothers and sister decided maybe it was time to come home once their commitments ran their course.

Noah turned onto First Street and then continued straight until the road unceremoniously turned into a gravel driveway that led toward his dad's place. The only marker that denoted the property line was the mailbox and the newspaper tube bolted to the pole underneath.

Gus had adamantly refused to sell the twenty acres of land after his wife died. He claimed that wasn't what she would have wanted. He was right, but that didn't mean his children wouldn't worry about him living a mile outside of town.

All of that would change now that they were all returning to their home of record.

Home of record was a military term; one of the first that a recruit learned when he or she joined the service. Anyone who enlisted in any of the services had to go to a city upstate where they had a place called MEPS. The Military Entrance and Processing Station (MEPS) was where one got all the paperwork done and, of course, the physical examination.

Each of his siblings would all be returning at staggered times, but that conclusion of their combined exodus would be reached within a year's time. Continuing the family legacy of serving their country had been important to all of them and instilled a sense of what was important in this life—God, family, country, and service.

The song on the radio cut off as the Bluetooth system was activated by his phone. He pressed the button on his steering wheel to accept the call, surprised at the name displayed on the screen.

"Mitch, is everything okay?" Noah asked as he slowed the truck down to compensate for the loose gravel drive. Why was his brother calling? Mitch was the oldest sibling of the Kendall clan. He also didn't let any of them forget that little known fact, either. "Aren't you still in Afghanistan?"

"I'm actually in CONUS as of zero four hundred this morning. I know it's the big day for you, so I was just checking in. How does it feel to be a lowlife civilian puke again?"

"It's too early to tell." Noah didn't believe for a second that Mitch was calling to *check in*. It wasn't unheard of for all his brothers to go months on end without touching base with one another. Their sister, Gwen, was a little different. She made it a point to reach out to them at least once a month, if not once a week. "I'm pulling up the drive now. Is there something I should know? Dad isn't the type to organize a lame ass party, so what am I missing?"

"You always were the suspicious one." Someone yelled Mitch's name in the background, so it didn't surprise Noah when his oldest brother took the out. "I've got to run, but tell Dad I'll call him later this week to see if you are assimilating back into the local tribe. I still need to schedule my TAP class, but I'm hoping to be home by the holidays with all my accumulated terminal leave."

"Have fun with that shit," Noah muttered, having already taken the class for the transition assistance program. The class was designed to help service members better acclimate to civilian life. "Word of advice, don't piss off the instructors. They're all retired Sergeant Majors. They've got some good gouge. They haven't forgotten where they came from."

It wasn't hard to miss his brother's laugh before the line disconnected. Noah had a bad rap for pissing off his instructors, and it was truly undeserved. It wasn't his fault that his fifth-grade teacher, Mrs. Cutler, sat in gum. He had fully intended to throw it away in the garbage can after recess was over.

His mother's favorite pine trees came into view, bringing a smile to his face. The full-bodied pines were planted on both sides of the gravel lane. She always said they reminded her of the holidays. It wasn't long before a two-story yellow house came into view with a wrap-around porch.

His dad had maintained the upkeep on the property pretty well, which couldn't have been easy at his age. The large pole barn to the right was where Gus had his workshop. His handmade furniture was well-prized throughout the area. The small business had been lucrative enough to keep his five children in clothes, put food on the table, and have a little left over for life's amenities.

Noah pulled his truck onto the concrete slab to the right of the house, right next to the old basketball court. A glance out the passenger side window showed the man himself.

Gus Kendall was larger than life, as always.

No one would have ever been able to tell that he was sixty-three years of age except the family doctor. He had developed heart problems in his early forties and he'd had a heart attack at the age of fifty-six. That only added on to the numerous reasons why it was time for the family to come together and help shoulder the load.

Gus allowed the screen door to close slowly behind him as he walked to the top of the three wooden steps that matched the color of the house. It wasn't lost on Noah that Gus had taken up his wife's post without her favorite dishtowel in hand. It was bittersweet, but this was the best homecoming he could have asked for.

"Welcome home, son."

Noah met his dad at the bottom of the steps. There was nothing sweeter than to hear those three words. It suddenly became hard to swallow, so he remained silent and held out his hand. His father took it and then pulled him close. They held each other a few seconds longer than they usually did, but Noah didn't doubt they were each thinking of the same woman.

"It's good to be home, Dad," Noah replied once he found his voice. He pulled away, surprised when his dad clapped him on the back and maintained his hold as they walked up the stairs. The workshop was where he was always most comfortable. "Don't tell me you made lunch."

"Why make lunch when Annie's Diner is a mile down the road? Her meatloaf always did rival your mother's, God rest her soul."

Noah walked in the house behind his dad, noticing that not a picture or piece of furniture was out of place. Nothing had changed since Mary Kendall had been laid to rest. The wall leading up the staircase was lined with family photographs, her lace doily was still draped over the dining room table, the china cabinet still held her grandmother's tableware, and the interior still held a scent of freshly picked lilacs filling the vase on the dining room table.

His mother's presence hung in the air, and it was a welcoming embrace.

"Mom always did say you had a crush on old Ms. Osburn," Noah laughed, knowing full well his dad never had a stray thought in his head when it came to his wife. Besides, Ms. Osburn had to be in her eighties by now. "You mentioned in our last phone conversation that she'd retired. Who is running the diner nowadays?"

Noah followed his dad through the long foyer that hosted an entryway table his dad had made in the workshop out back a decade or two ago. Pretty much the entire house was filled with furniture made by his father. The kitchen table was more solid than any other table anyone could find in any furniture store. It had survived five children for thirty-four years.

He recounted, just to be sure he was right. Yes, Mitch was thirty-four years old and Lance was the youngest at twenty-nine. Noah shook his head in astonishment as to the strength his mother had to have in birthing five children in five years.

"Annie's daughter, Cassie, is currently running the diner. And let me tell you, she learned right quick that her fancy city dishes weren't going to cut it here in Blyth Lake," Gus grumbled as he poured two cups of coffee in the same mugs that had been in the cupboard since Noah was a little boy. "Meat and potatoes have always been the staple of a healthy living here in the Midwest. Speaking of which, I bought us some ribeye steaks to grill out tonight with a couple of spuds. I've got to say, it'll be nice having all you kids home."

"That reminds me. Mitch called." Noah looked out the kitchen window, catching sight of the tire swing still attached to the large maple tree out back. He'd fallen off it many times, but only once had he required stitches after ramming it into the tree. That was all because of a dare Mitch had made that Noah couldn't get it to spin the fastest. "He's stateside and thinking he should be home for the holidays."

"That's better than he first thought. Lance is thinking he'll be home next month, and then Gwen the month after."

Gus brought both mugs over to the kitchen table before pulling out a chair. He motioned for Noah to do the same, but he shook his head at the offer. He needed to stretch his legs after such a long drive.

"Are you sure you're ready to have the house overflowing with all us kids again?"

Noah was only half-kidding. Only one of them was certain as to what their future held. That was Gwen. She'd served in the Navy and had gotten out around four years prior. She finished her bachelor's degree within two years and was a very successful personal financial advisor. She'd already scoped out an office on Main Street, right next to the only bank in town.

"About that," Gus started to say before pausing, settling himself in the same chair he used at every meal. The seat was positioned at the head of the table, but it also provided him a view of the entire kitchen. Noah hadn't understood it as a boy, but the military had ingrained a specific conduct in his father that had saved countless lives—never expose your back. "Take a seat, son. There's something we need to discuss."

Noah's initial reaction was to refuse. Nothing good ever came from when his father uttered the words *take a seat, son.* Memories from when he *borrowed* the truck or when he had stolen a beer out of the refrigerator on one of Lance's dares came to mind. Come to think of it, the majority of the shit he got himself into came from dares his brothers had dreamed up.

"Is everyone alright?"

Noah took his time crossing the kitchen tile. He wasn't in any hurry to receive another blow. The news of his mother's death had been more than enough.

"Everyone is fine." Gus lifted a keyring off the kitchen table and took his time removing one of the keys off the metal sphere. It was then Noah noticed a gleam of excitement in his father's eyes, along with what appeared to be sorrow. "Do you remember your grandfather?"

"Grandpa Earl? Sure, I do," Noah replied, recalling his mother's father giving all the boys a silver dollar when he walked into the house every Sunday afternoon for dinner. Gwen always received two dollars, which she took great pride in rubbing in her brother's faces. "I must have been, what? Ten years old when he died?"

"That sounds about right." Gus finally worked the key off the silver ring. He set it on the table and slowly pushed it toward Noah. It couldn't have been a key to the house, because he already had one. "Earl and I sometimes didn't quite see eye to eye on things, though I respected the man for who he was."

"You mean the time he wanted to buy you and Mom a new vehicle when the truck broke down?" Again, there were certain things a young boy didn't understand until he was older. His father was a very proud man. He supported his wife and family without any help from others…including family. "It took you two days to fix that old Ford. Mitch had to walk to and from football practice on his own."

"It did him good," Gus said gruffly, emotion heavy in his tone. He gestured toward the key, still on the table. "Anyway, your grandfather left a sizable inheritance for your mother when he passed. We never touched a penny of it. It sat in the bank collecting interest until just before your mother's passing."

"Wait," Noah directed, thinking back to when his mom and uncle went months without speaking to one another. "Is that why Uncle Jimmy stopped coming to Sunday dinner?"

Noah had always assumed it was too hard on Jim Webb to be surrounded by family when he didn't have one of his own. Losing Grandpa Earl had been difficult on everyone.

"That about sums it up. Your uncle was cut out of Earl's will because of how he disgraced the family name." Gus took a drink of his coffee, taking his time to formulate an answer. Noah braced himself, never liking family secrets. The last one had been finding out that Uncle Jimmy had done a stint in jail. "It all stemmed from when your uncle stole some valuables from your grandparent's house instead of telling them he needed the money. It only got worse when Jimmy refused to get help for his drinking problem."

Jim Webb had always been the black sheep of the family, but Noah felt for the man. Living in Grandpa Earl's shadow couldn't have been easy.

"Your mother never doubted that each of you boys would return home at some point in your lives." Gus set his mug down on the table with a smile. "Mary wasn't so sure about Gwen, though. That girl never did like being smothered by you boys when it came to her boyfriends."

"Gwen doesn't seem to have a problem being the one to suffocate us," Noah reminded his dad wryly. "Have you received your monthly call?"

"She rings me weekly," Gus answered with a smile, the pride for his daughter shining through. "I don't want you ruining this moment for the others, so keep that in mind the next time she calls you."

"Ruin what?"

"Your mother bought each of you a parcel of property here

in Blyth Lake." Gus leaned forward and planted an elbow on the table. He tapped the key with his other hand. "She used the money from her inheritance to buy you a home. You got the old Yoder farm. Having you all come home was her final wish, son."

CHAPTER THREE

"I WISH YOU'D take a real vacation instead of wasting your time in Blyth Lake."

Reese Woodward stared down at the worn notebook in her hand, counting at least seven names on her list. An additional three had already been scratched out as dead ends. One of the remaining individuals had the answers she was seeking.

"I can't do this with you right now, Tanner." Reese tossed the small notebook on the counter with a sense of purpose. "Emma Irwin went missing twelve years ago. One year to the day before Sophia disappeared. I know there's a connection. That photograph proved it."

"No," Tanner argued, saying the same thing he'd said in their previous conversation. "You *want* there to be a connection, so you've convinced yourself there is one. Everyone back then attended the same summer camps within a sixty-mile vicinity. Hell, even I went that year, not that I remember Emma at all. All you're doing is wasting your money skulking around some backwater town."

Reese grabbed the glass of sweet iced tea she'd made this morning and pushed open the screen door. The afternoon temperature was rising and it was already well into the mid-eighties. She'd heard over the radio this morning that tomorrow would be even hotter.

The humidity wasn't that much different out here on the

porch than it was inside the house. Unfortunately, the rental had no central air conditioning unit. Just a fan. Unless there was a cross breeze, not even the open windows could keep the place cool in the heat of the day.

She didn't really mind. The sun was shining, the birds were singing, and the wildflowers had already bloomed. Summer had officially arrived, and with it a new sense of purpose.

Reese had an opportunity here to find out what had happened to Sophia all those years ago.

"I'm not wasting a dime. I'm on vacation," Reese reminded her cousin, stepping over a rotted board in the floor. Other than that one decaying plank, the porch was quite solid. She took a seat on the porch swing she suspected had been hung here fifty years prior and lifted her face to the slightest of breezes. She slowly drew in a breath, savoring the sweet scent of summer that hung in the air. "There's really no difference between spending money in Ohio versus renting a house in Florida at astronomical prices. In fact, I'm saving money."

"If you think that, then I know you've gone batshit crazy."

Reese could picture Tanner rubbing his forehead the way he did when he was frustrated with her logic. They might only be cousins, but they were more like brother and sister, considering how they were raised. Their mothers were sisters who lived in the same small town of Heartland, Ohio. There wasn't a day that went by when they weren't visiting each other's houses for one reason or another.

"Sophia didn't run away, Tanner. She wouldn't have done that to us. You know her." Reese didn't want to get into another argument with her cousin, so she switched topics. Eleven years had passed since Sophia had been declared a runaway. The sharp pain of abandonment had eventually turned into a dull heartache, and even that only materialized when her name was mentioned at holidays and family outings. Time had a way of erasing the pain and only promoting the cherished memories. "Have you talked to your mom recently? I thought about driving over there this weekend, but then I'd have to answer too many questions about where I had been. Mom said that Aunt Lydia cut and styled her hair. It's the talk of the town."

Reese and Tanner had both agreed not to tell their families what she was doing in Blyth Lake. She was only around thirty miles from their hometown, but she lived and taught algebra at a high school in Springfield, Illinois. She'd had to go where the teaching jobs were upon graduating from Ohio State University.

Unfortunately, driving to her parent's house meant spending more than just the weekend. She loved her family, but Tanner didn't have to endure the guilt trip she got for being so far from home every time she showed up for a holiday. He still resided in their tiny hometown of Heartland and had dinner with the family every Sunday.

"I spoke to Mom yesterday. She's gearing up to have one of her garage sales." Tanner paused, as if it suddenly dawned on him what that meant for his childhood memories. "Awww, damn it. Let me call you back tonight. I'm just now wondering what she's got her hands on."

Reese smiled as Tanner disconnected the line, no doubt calling his mom to make sure she didn't include his autographed CD of Green Day's *American Idiot* or any of his other prized collection of junk he kept at the house. The CD was his favorite from when they were teenagers. He must have shown it to half the town. Her grin faded as she recalled Sophia's love for the popular band, as well.

Sophia hadn't run away from home, regardless of what the police had thought at the time. Something had happened to her. Something bad had come to visit their small town.

Reese sighed as she slipped her cell phone in between her legs. She pushed off the porch with her flip-flop to put the swing in motion, thinking maybe she should have shared with Tanner that this break was becoming rejuvenating in a strange sort of way. She'd gotten so caught up in the same monotonous daily routine back in Springfield that she was beginning to lose sight of who she was and what she wanted for her future.

She still wasn't completely sure about the latter.

Technically, this was the best vacation she could have asked for. The stillness out here in the country held a peaceful quality that one couldn't find nor buy in the city. It made her think that maybe it was time she moved back home to take a job at her old high school.

The distant sound of a heavy vehicle reached her well before she caught sight of a dusty black F150 driving down the dirt road. The driver wasn't speeding at all, but the ground hadn't seen rain in well over two weeks.

The road was basically rock, and it had been oiled in the past, but that had to have been over a year past considering all the dirt one kicked up when driving it now. A cloud of dust followed closely behind the bed of the truck as it passed by the flat stretch of her front lawn. The house she'd rented was set back a good ways from the road.

There was only one destination that the vehicle could be headed to, and that was nothing but a ramshackle old farmhouse a half mile down the old rock road.

Why?

It was a shame that the county had allowed a picturesque property to slip in such a way. It was now basically derelict. Okay, she might be exaggerating a bit, but the house needed more than just an update. It needed a total renovation to become livable.

Hell, the electrical and plumbing had to be from the last century. She wondered if it wouldn't be easier to just knock it down and start over.

She'd heard the last owners had walked out on the mortgage around five years ago after being unable to sell off the farmland. Word had it that some of the high school kids still hung out there when they skipped school or wanted to have a party. She'd seen no evidence of that kind of behavior in the past week that she'd been renting here, though.

Reese hadn't heard any music or loud voices coming from that direction. Then again, high school was out for the summer and folks were on vacation to typical places like Florida. The kids who were still stuck at home were most likely hanging out at the lake across town—the girls in their bikinis and the boys staring at them from behind their mirrored sunglasses.

The teens wouldn't need a place to hide their drinking parties until school started back up in late August and fall started to set in.

Reese glanced to her left even though various pines and oak trees prevented her from seeing the house or the old barn. Her daily jog always took her out past the property to the dead end at the edge of the woods bordering the DNR wetlands preserve, because the other direction led to one of the main roads that had too much traffic for her liking.

Come to think of it, she had seen some old discarded beer cans out there at the turnaround, along with some old rusting junk folks had thrown down there.

She'd never caught sight of anyone trespassing or even taking the shortcut back through the cluster of woods that led to Seventh Street. The road they were on paralleled the edge of town, maybe a half mile away. The woods between them and the town were covered in game trails and uneven broken ground, especially near the small creek. Well, it was according to the map she'd looked over the other day.

That area was only a hop, skip, and a jump from Seventh to hit Main Street once you crossed through the woods.

It was hard for her to put a finger on it, but there was something sinister about the old farm property. It could have easily been the fact that there were a couple of windows missing or the fact that the screen door was hanging on by just one hinge. It resembled one of those deserted houses in the movies where the kids always dared each other to spend the night and talked about ghosts.

Either way, she only ever ventured that direction during the morning hours when she was running.

She never went out there after dark, and never at night.

It was probably all in her head. Reese had spent too much time reading about Emma Irwin's disappearance. The young girl was last seen at a party on the very same Yoder farm. At least, that's what it was called back then. It still was. Old habits died hard.

Regardless, the latest owners had moved in months after Emma had basically vanished into thin air, just like Reese's cousin had a year later. Emma Irwin had never once given the impression that she wanted to run away, though some had said she'd gotten pregnant and the family had snuck her out of town.

The sheriff had first treated her disappearance as a kidnapping, so unlike Sophia's case where the police had ruled her as a runaway. The police had conducted searches for Emma and played out the whole campaign to locate her.

Neither girl had ever been found.

Not a trace.

That couldn't be a coincidence, could it?

Was Tanner right? Was she just wishing there was a connection?

Was she wasting time here, looking for a correlation where there was none?

She'd already decided to head into town for dinner, but she also had every intention of driving her car. Now, curiosity got the better of her. A walk might do her some good. Besides, she'd be able to return home before dusk.

Why was someone visiting the Yoder's place, anyway? Had the property finally been sold?

Reese suppressed a shiver at the thought of someone moving into such a dreary place. To each their own, but she couldn't help but wonder if it was a local or another out-of-towner who bought the place for the land value.

She stood and slid her cell phone into the back pocket of her shorts. It was a beautiful day. It wouldn't hurt to use the shortcut into town. Surely she'd be back before it got too dark, and the little hike would allow her to see what was going on next door.

Not that she was being nosey or anything. Furthermore, Annie's Diner always brought in a lot of local traffic. It was still early, but there should be some patrons rattling around the place. And who knows, she might get lucky. Maybe another name could be crossed off her list.

It hadn't been that hard to acquire the names of those who attended the camp Emma and Sophia had gone to that summer. Two of the women had moved away after their high school graduation, and one of the men had unfortunately died in a freak skiing accident two years back. That left seven people who might have a clue as to why Emma and Sophia went missing within a year of each other.

Reese quickly walked back into the house and set her glass of iced tea in the fridge before grabbing her keys. She hesitated, thinking she might want to close all the windows before leaving.

She decided against it. The last time she closed and secured all the windows, she might as well have lived in the bottom of a volcano that night.

She locked the door behind her, figuring the screens were set in place. Regardless of what had happened twelve years ago, the worst crime to be committed in Blyth Lake was a couple of teenagers being picked up for four-wheeling through a farmer's pasture and scaring his herd half to death just north of town. There had been some mention of vandalism being done to the abandoned house next door, but no one had ever confessed, leaving the sheriff nothing to go on other than some graffiti.

Reese hooked her keys onto the belt loop of her jean shorts and patted her back pocket where she'd stored a twenty-dollar bill, her identification, and a credit card before descending the stairs. She walked down the gravel driveway to the rock road, all the while peering to the left to see if the truck was coming back her way. It wasn't.

The only sounds she heard were the birds and two chipmunks chasing each other into the cluster of trees. Her mind spun with ideas as to why someone would want to buy the property next door when it had been deserted for so long. It was foolish of her to think it might have something to do with Emma's disappearance, but she could rationalize just about anything at this point.

Reese chalked it up to too many hours in front of the computer researching missing children and the unspeakable crimes people committed on them. She was letting her mind run away with her, so the best thing would be for her to walk past the property and find out for herself why someone would want to purchase a rundown house out past the edge of town.

CHAPTER FOUR

NOAH PUSHED OPEN the driver's side door of his truck, but he didn't exit the cab. He stared in disbelief at the massive neglect this house had experienced, questioning why his parents had purchased this place for his homecoming.

He wasn't ungrateful in the least.

It was just hard for him to wrap his mind around the fact that his parents had a nest egg they could have used a million times over during the course of their marriage for any number of things.

Instead, they'd chosen to save it for their children.

He didn't doubt for a minute that his father's pride contributed to that decision, but the result was the same. Mary Kendall had gotten her wish—to have her family close at hand.

"It's bittersweet."

"Yes," Gus acknowledged after clearing his throat a couple times. "Yes, it is."

Gus got out of the cab and shut the door, walking around the truck so that he could lean against the front bumper. He crossed his arms and stared at the broken windows, the red spray paint across the porch windows proclaiming the property as *Douchebag Manor*, and the cavalcade of broken planks that hadn't gotten that way with age.

Noah saw the surface damage, but there was so much potential here. The two-story farmhouse sat on a good thirty acres of open pastures that butted up against the DNR land to the east and was separated from the town to the west by a half-mile of hardwood forest. Though it had always been called Yoder's farm, it wasn't technically farmland. The Yoders had kept a couple of horses, a medium-sized herd of dairy cows, and a mess of chickens on the property fifteen years or so back, mostly growing a patch of pumpkins and squash for additional money in the fall season.

Phil Yoder's death had been unexpected. The family carried on with their small dairy farm for a time after his passing. It wasn't a surprise to the town when his former wife and her older children moved east to stay with family when their *Ordnung* of the Amish moved out of the area back to Pennsylvania. It was the following football season that this place had turned into party central.

Gus probably had no idea, but Noah's first kiss with Beth Ann Mason had been up in the hayloft of the old barn located at the back of the house near the pond. They'd had their legs dangling out over the second-story doorway the farmhands had once used to load hay. He remembered staring down at the bonfire, watching as it reflected off the pond when he'd made his move.

She'd broken his heart the next day when he saw her wearing Chad Schaeffer's letterman's jacket.

Noah removed the keys from the ignition before joining his father, curious as to why the previous homeowners had left town.

"How long has it been since the Andersons moved?"

"About five years, give or take a bit. Pete got a good-paying job down in Texas. It was too good to pass up, but he couldn't sell the property for what he was asking."

"So Pete just hung on to it?" Noah asked, thinking that was

a long time to go paying a second mortgage, including property taxes and all.

"Unfortunately, he eventually let the farmhouse and land go into foreclosure. It went up for auction around a year ago." Gus nodded back toward town. "I bought Harlan Whitmore a bottle of scotch not to spread the word that I'd put in a bid. I didn't want you kids to hear that I'd been buying up a number of properties in Blyth Lake. Your mother was very clear with her instructions. I had the place put in your name last week. You're on the hook for property taxes next year. It's all yours now."

"I won't ruin this surprise for the others. You have my word." Noah was curious about something, though. "Have all the other properties been purchased?"

"You'll find out when your brothers and sister find out," Gus said pointedly, shooting Noah a stern look as he bit down on the toothpick he'd taken from the shot glass he kept full of them on his kitchen table. He was usually always one step ahead of his children. "You realize the house is going to need a new roof...like yesterday, right?"

"New windows, insulation, and siding," Noah contributed to the list of renovations. "The porch needs more than a little work, but it could technically be expanded around either side or both. I suspect I'll be changing the name of the place. The red spray paint just clashes."

"Wraparound?" Gus inquired, moving the toothpick to the other side of his mouth as he smiled in reference to the nickname the local teens had given the place. "You might consider screening in the porch with that pond so close by. The mosquitoes have only gotten worse over the years. Hell, it's going to take a bulldozer to muck out the moss that's grown over the surface. That is, where the cattails haven't taken over."

Noah leaned back and reached into the front of his jeans for the key his father had given him earlier this afternoon. He held it up before twisting it around in reverence.

"Twelve years in the Marines, and I've always stayed in the bachelor quarters or the barracks." Noah shook his head at the responsibility laid out in front of him. His fingers itched to get started. "I never in a million years imagined this kind of project."

"You're not disappointed, are you?"

Noah had to have heard wrong, but he realized his dad had asked the question in all seriousness. Even a slight tension had settled in his shoulders, almost as if he expected some type of rejection.

Noah suspected one of his dad's old buddies might have suggested over a beer or two that not all his kids would be happy with this type of gift.

They were wrong.

"Dad, there isn't a single kid of yours that will come home and be disappointed at what's waiting for them...and that includes me." Noah shook his head in wonderment. He held up the key a little higher. "I finally have a place to call my own. You always taught us that hard work pays off. By the time I get done with her, she'll be restored back to her old glory days...even better."

Noah wasn't sure what made him look over his shoulder, because he certainly didn't have the best hearing after twelve years in the service. Tinnitus had set in after his second combat tour, leaving behind a constant ringing that no longer bothered him more out of habit than comfort. It was astonishing what the human body could withstand over multiple years of torture.

"Dad, who is that?"

A beautiful woman was casually walking toward the shortcut he remembered very well from his youth. She flashed a smile his way and waved her hand casually in greeting, but she didn't veer from her destination. It appeared she was taking the shortcut he knew would lead her into town.

"Her name is Reese Woodward. She's renting out Rose Phifer's cottage for the summer. She grew up around here. Heartland, I think."

Reese. The name seemed fitting, reminding him of that blonde actress who always starred in those romantic comedies. Her hair was piled high on top of her head in what his sister always referred to as a messy bun. Her hair wasn't blonde, but rather a light shade of chestnut.

A pair of oversized sunglasses with dark brown lenses sat high up on the bridge of her nose. She had on a pair of denim shorts, but they were still long enough to leave his imagination running wild.

She was downright stunning.

Things were looking up around here.

"Really?" Noah asked, as he watched Reese disappear into the woods. An uneasiness settled over him as he thought back to a night he hadn't thought about in years. "Why would she rent a house in Blyth Lake?"

"You'd have to ask her that yourself, son." Gus' tone suggested that he thought Noah would do just that. "Now, let's go take a look at the inside of your new home improvement project. We can tour the outside after you find out about the electric and plumbing problems."

Noah dragged his gaze away from where Reese had vanished from view. He'd probably be smart to stay away, considering he'd just gotten back to town. He hadn't even had time to hit up the local watering hole where he had no doubt some of his old friends were still gathered.

Gus had decided to grill up the steaks for lunch instead of dinner. The two had talked for hours before finally deciding to take a drive across town to see the new place. They'd more than likely hit up the diner in an hour or so.

"Let's do this," Noah said excitedly, pushing aside the curiosity he had about Reese Woodward. It was none of his business who she was and why she was visiting Blyth Lake. "I remember this place being renovated twelve years ago. I hope the Andersons left the hardwood floors intact."

"You'll be disappointed then," Gus warned, maneuvering around the broken wooden step. "I had an inspector check to see if there were any problems with the foundation. Turns out the Andersons had a penchant for shag carpeting."

Noah suppressed a groan as he slid the key inside the deadbolt, turning until the latch slid free of its home. There were only one or two broken windows from the front of the house. It hadn't been enough to let the air pass through. The stifling heat was somewhat overwhelming as Noah stepped over the threshold...onto what had most likely once been cream shag carpet.

"You weren't kidding. This is horrible." Noah wasn't impressed with the Andersons' taste in design, but his memories were from a different time. He took in the large living room, already having a picture in his mind's eye as to what his home could become. "There's got to be some hardwood left underneath this carpet. And look up there. They painted the exposed beams a beige color to match the walls. What the hell were they thinking?"

Gus walked over to a corner of the living room, peeling back an upturned piece of carpet. He nodded his agreement.

"You're right. That's some fine-looking flooring under this crap." Gus removed the toothpick from in between his lips before standing, gesturing toward the exposed beams near the ceiling. "How did you know the Andersons painted that wood and not the Yoders?'"

Noah shot his dad a look of skepticism. Was he being seri-ous?

"Dad, you know very well we used this place to have parties every Saturday night. We never did anything like what these kids do nowadays." Noah took in the broken pane of glass in the windowsill on the far side of the wall. "We mainly used the abandoned firewood pile to make a bonfire and used the barn for...well, you know. Anyway, a group of us came back here the morning after Emma Irwin went missing. We joined the search party, remember that?"

"I do," Gus replied, shaking his head in regret. "That poor girl and her family. It's a parent's worst nightmare."

Noah took another step closer to the window, looking out toward the woods in the direction Reese had taken. Billy Stanton had said he last saw Emma taking that same route, but nothing had ever come of it. There were a lot of theories as to what had happened to her, but none had ever been proven out worth a damn.

Emma Irwin had never been seen after that night.

"I never thought about what happened back then when buying this property," Gus admitted, crossing his arms as he looked around the room. "It happened so long ago."

"I have good memories here, Dad." Noah was telling the truth. His first kiss had taken place right here on this patch of ground, as did reaching second base with Whitney Bell shortly thereafter. He, his brothers, and most of their friends had some of their best times here. "Emma disappearing that night had nothing to do with this place. Do you remember Uncle Jimmy saying he thought he saw her walking down Seventh Street? Whatever happened to her didn't occur here."

Noah didn't want to think back to that confusing and emotional time. Emma had been a year younger, but they still ran in the same circles. Months and months of his senior year had been consumed with the mystery of her disappearance.

As with anything, though, the years had faded the pain for the entire town—with the exception of her family, of course.

"What is that?" Noah asked, realizing that the far wall had never been between the living room and the kitchen. He closed the distance, passing his father so that he could see what the Andersons had done with the layout. "This used to open up into the kitchen. Remember?"

"Pete wanted an office, so he used the small space that was for the dining room and closed it off." Gus didn't bother to go into the office. His attention was on the kitchen. "If you take down those two walls, you'd be able to install a rather large island where the family can congregate around when making Sunday dinner."

"Sunday dinner will always take place at your house, Dad. You know that." That didn't mean Noah wouldn't host Thursday night football games with his brothers and sister coming over to watch the Browns play the Steelers. That rivalry went way back. Leave it to Gwen to be the only one of them to support a rival team. He was sure that was entirely by design. "But I see what you mean. These two walls take up too much space."

"I was talking about your own family, son."

Noah let that comment slide, not knowing what the future held for him. He and his dad walked through the entire house noting numerous problems before venturing outside, touring the property and ensuring the barn was still sturdy. It could use some of that new metal siding and a new roof to give it a chance at lasting a while longer.

Gus most likely had already inspected all this before purchasing the property, but he kept up the front of interest as Noah made mental notes about what needed to be done and what should come first.

"You know, I was thinking." Noah turned around, walking backwards as he took one last look at the house. "If I buy some boards to put over the broken windows, I could technically stay here."

"I'm not going to listen to that horseshit." Gus motioned for Noah to get into the truck with a sharp wave of his hand. "You'll stay with me. No reason you shouldn't sleep in a comfortable bed while you whip this place into shape. Now, let's get to Annie's before that fine meatloaf runs out."

"I take it Cassie didn't change that particular recipe?"

Noah settled back behind the wheel and turned over the engine while Gus talked about a revolt that almost took place a year ago when Annie's daughter moved back into town. He hadn't meant to tune his dad out, but his thoughts drifted to all the renovations he wanted to get started on tomorrow morning.

"Noah? I'm not gonna be real pleased if I don't get my meat-loaf."

His parents had given him the ability to build his own home. It was hard to put into words the gratitude flowing through him.

"Dad, I—"

"I know, son," Gus said with a pat on Noah's shoulder. "I know. Enough said."

CHAPTER FIVE

REESE SAT BACK as the waitress set a piece of homemade apple pie on the laminate-covered tabletop in front of her.

Of course, a 1950s styled restaurant wouldn't be complete without those telltale tables with the chrome trim. It was more than apparent the management had recently redecorated this place in a retro theme.

Annie's Diner was decked out with all the trimmings, right down to the Seeburg Wall-O-Matic tableside jukeboxes. The music selection was rather limited to the songs from that era, but the way the pictures of James Dean, Elvis, and the V-E Day *Kissing Sailor* adorned the walls tended to put one in a nostalgic frame of mind.

One thing was for sure, the comfort food that was their staple was beyond amazing. She smothered a groan as her stomach protested the thought of taking one more bite, but the delicious cinnamon aroma was just too tempting.

She reached for her fork.

"It's a good thing I walked here," Reese muttered to herself right before she lifted the small bite to her lips. The sweet sugary flavor burst onto her tongue with the unabashed pride of the cook. "Unbelievable."

"I'm glad you like it," Cassie laughed from the booth she occupied in front of Reese. "I used my mom's recipe and added a couple of ingredients I thought would bring out the flavors of the Granny Smith apples."

"Whatever you used works for me."

"Just don't tell my mother," Cassie warned with a wink.

"That reminds me, Darcy called a few minutes ago. He's taking your mother into the city later this week for a doctor's appointment," the waitress said as she made her way back around the counter. Her name tag read Molly, and she and Reese had been on first name basis ever since she'd set foot in this quaint little diner. "He wanted me to tell you that he's stopping by later today to pick up her insurance card."

"Crap," Cassie muttered, dropping her pen on the papers. "I forgot that I had those from her last visit. At least he'll be the one to deal with Mama's pigheadedness when it comes to Dr. Stanton telling her she's got to take her blood pressure medication regularly. I try to get her to take it the same time every day."

Reese took another bite as the bell above the door chimed, indicating another customer. A quick glance over Cassie's head revealed Harlan Whitmore. He was a local real estate agent. It was hard to mistake him, considering his mug was plastered on a billboard alongside the road coming into town.

Technically, Harlan was the only choice in town for real estate, but at least a resident could select from either First Federal or Union Bank for banking. There had been some talk of a credit union having occupied some space on Main Street, but that went away when the mill shut down.

Cassie stood and collected the mounds of paperwork she'd been working on for the past forty-five minutes. Business must be good from the way she was smiling and talking with each person who walked in the door. She cleared the way for Harlan in case he wanted a booth instead of one of the tables, but he chose a stool at the counter instead.

"I hear Noah Kendall is back in town," Calvin Arlo said

after Harlan had taken the stool next to him. He never looked to his left as he sat down or else he would have recognized Reese. Harlan was the person she'd gone to regarding her rental. As for Calvin, he owned the hardware store located on the other end of Main Street and came here every day for lunch. "You might have a new customer, Whitmore."

"God knows I could use it," Harlan mumbled, turning over the white porcelain coffee cup in front of him. "Practically every town and city in Ohio has seen an uptick in real estate recently. You'd think the same could be said for Blyth Lake, but that just isn't the case."

"That's because everyone is packing up and taking jobs in the cities. The service industry is all that's left. Look at Cassie. That's what she did all those years ago. The only reason she's back is to take care of her mother's business. As for all these other younger folks? Hell, they wouldn't know how to change the oil in their own car if their lives depended on it. God help them if they needed to change a tire without roadside service." Calvin nodded to Molly when she hovered the pot of coffee over his mug after having filled Harlan's. "I have brand new tool sets that are collecting dust in the back of my store because no one wants to get their hands dirty anymore."

"The usual, Harlan?" Molly set the glass carafe back on the burner before pulling out an order pad from her apron. "With or without gravy today?"

Reese continued to observe the two men quietly as they picked up their conversation after Harlan had agreed to the extra brown gravy over his meatloaf. She realized that he never truly answered Calvin's question regarding the possibility of a new client. Harlan was right about the real estate around here, though. The older properties were definitely a harder sell to the younger set.

She'd been waiting for the right time to speak with Calvin, but the diner had been too quiet. Anyone here would have been able to hear their entire conversation. She would have to come up with a reason to stop by the hardware store this week. Maybe she could pick up a roadside emergency kit. She could just imagine the look on his face if she did that. Her father had long since taught her how to change a tire, do an oil change, and set the points properly on a dwell meter.

Calvin was in his early sixties with greying hair, but seemed like a nice enough guy. He'd been one of the counselors at the camp Sophia and Emma had attended twelve years ago. It was possible that he remembered something back then that would shed light on why two girls from the same summer camp went missing exactly twelve months of apart from one another.

Reese wasn't kidding herself that she would find either one of them alive and well. It was more of a personal goal to prove to her family that Sophia hadn't run away like everyone seemed to think. Even Aunt Lydia had finally yielded to the pressure regarding that theory, which was why Sophia's room remained intact. Aunt Lydia still held out hope that Sophia would eventually return home someday like she'd just forgotten where they lived or something.

"You okay, darlin'?"

Reese glanced up to find Molly looking at her with concern.

"I'm still trying to figure out where I'm going to fit this," Reese said without missing a beat. She used the side of the fork prongs to cut off another bite of pie.

"You could use a pound or two, if you ask me." Molly smiled down at her as she rested one hand on her hip, looking as if she planned to stay awhile. "You never did say why you chose Blyth Lake to take your summer vacation. Seems to me that you might find more to do in the city."

Some of the conversations taking place around the diner slowed down or stopped altogether. Reese was very familiar with how small towns worked, and the gossip mill was waiting on more grist for the stone to churn out another fresh story to the other gossipmongers among them. It was why she'd been very careful on how she worded her questions about Sophia.

It was only natural that the townsfolk were curious about her, but she hadn't wanted to reveal the real reason she was here. Blyth Lake's residents were protective of one another, rightfully so, just as they were in Heartland. What she wanted to find out was if a werewolf might be lurking around seeking out the defenseless lambs among the gentle sheep.

Yes, that sounded dramatic, but it was true nonetheless.

It looked as if she would have to come clean though, because she wouldn't lie to these good people either. She had just parted her lips to share her story when the bell above the door chimed again.

The diner erupted in loud greetings and even some heartfelt applause.

Reese watched as the two men, who were at the old Yoder farm, entered the diner, the younger one taking the attention in stride with a bit of a flush. He greeted every patron as if they were family, even suffering through the quick embraces and pecks on the cheek from some of the older ladies.

Who was this man and why was everyone treating him like a rock star?

"If it isn't Noah Kendall," Cassie sang loudly as she came through the swinging doors. Her entrance had been timed perfectly. Noah had just finished greeting everyone right when the middle-aged woman stepped into his path, wrapping her arms around his neck. She'd quite obviously taken him by surprise. Reese had thought of Cassie as a downhome country girl who chose to spend her money on fashion. Now? A cougar had emerged, with shiny fangs and all. "Well, don't you look as handsome as ever, darlin'."

"Oh, I don't know about that. More worse for wear, I'd say."

Noah had one of those rich voices that sent shivers down a girl's back. He'd shifted a bit to escape the woman's forward embrace. It was then that his startling blue eyes met hers and held them for just that singular moment, just enough time to spark a fire in her soul.

Reese hadn't meant to draw attention to herself, but his sudden wink had her fumbling the fork in her hand.

"Can I finally share the news, Gus?" Harlan had turned on his stool, respectfully waiting his turn. He held out his hand to Noah in welcome. "Good to see you, Noah."

"Likewise," Noah greeted, finally allowing Reese to breathe a little as he diverted his attention to the real estate agent. There was something about him that stole all the oxygen from the room. "And yes, Dad and I just came back from looking over the old Yoder farmhouse."

"The Noah Kendall place now," Harlan announced to everyone, puffing out his chest as he broadcasted one of his latest sales. "Congratulations."

"Thank you, Harlan."

The older man standing behind Noah had to be his father. They were almost the same height, shared the same handsome features, and there was a proudness in the way his gaze rested on Noah that only a parent could own.

Reese did her best to blend in with the booth as she continued to watch what appeared to be some kind of traditional homecoming. She took another bite of her apple pie, observing and listening to what was going on around her.

Kendall. She recalled seeing the Kendall surname on her list of people who had attended the camp with Sophia, but the first name had been Lance. Maybe they were brothers?

"You think that was a greeting?" Gus muttered as he claimed the booth in front of Reese. His back was to her, which meant Noah was now facing her. Reese averted her gaze down to what was left of her apple pie. She didn't want to get caught eavesdropping. "You just wait until we hit Tiny's Cavern tonight. Your old crowd still hangs out there every Thursday night."

"I want to stop by Calvin's hardware store to pick up some wood for the windows before hitting Tiny's. I don't like leaving the house exposed like that. It's about time I put the town's teenagers on notice that the place isn't open season any longer for their tags. *Douchebag Manor* is closed for business."

Reese wanted to join in their conversation and tell Noah Kendall that he should probably just flip the property rather than sink too much money into the place. Harlan was still at the counter waiting on his meatloaf. There wasn't anything wrong with admitting mistakes, and in her opinion, Noah had made a huge one.

There was something very dark about that farmhouse at the end of the road.

The two men continued to talk about what work needed to be done on the house first before turning to family matters. It didn't surprise her to find out that Noah was returning home after serving twelve years in the Marines. His entire demeanor, the way he carried himself, and the way his gaze had taken in every patron in the place had told her he was a warrior—either military, law enforcement, or both.

Noah's black hair was cut in a traditional high and tight, similar to the way her uncle had kept his styled for years after he retired from the Army. Uncle Theo also had some pretty high standards to live up to, which had always been a point of contention between him and his children. Tanner had eventually fallen into line, but Sophia had rebelled with her whole heart.

"You never did get around to saying why you chose Blyth Lake as the place for your summer vacation." Molly really needed to scrape the soles of her shoes or something. This was the second time she'd snuck up on Reese. The cheerful, yet prying, waitress slid the check on the table while she waited for Reese to answer. "You have relatives around these parts?"

"Um, no, not really," Reese replied, delaying the inevitable as she used the white napkin to wipe away the nonexistent crumbs on her lips. She wasn't sure why she looked in Noah's direction, but she couldn't say she was surprised he was waiting for her answer with the rest of the diner. Here went nothing. "I actually grew up in Heartland, around thirty miles from here. I'm in town because of—"

"Well, if it ain't my favorite nephew."

Reese was once again saved from answering Molly's question when a man's voice echoed throughout the diner. Reese hadn't heard the bell chime as she had been fortifying herself for what could very well turn out to be animosity in attempting to dig up the past. She was here for the summer, so she'd been taking it slow in bringing up Emma Irwin's disappearance while seeking the answers she sought. It appeared she'd been given a little more time.

"Uncle Jimmy." Noah slid out from the booth and offered his hand to a male who wasn't quite as tall and didn't resemble the Kendall men in any way. Reese wondered if maybe Jimmy wasn't the brother of Noah's mother rather than his dad. It would explain the lighter hair and more hawkish features. "It's been a while."

"Three years, near as I can figure." Jimmy didn't so much as look in Gus' direction. Tension had settled over the diner, and it was obvious there was some bad blood between these family members. Noah didn't seem at all bothered by it, though. "I hear you're back home for good."

"I am," Noah replied, shifting out of the way so that Cassie could set their drink order down on the table. It was unusual to see her waiting on tables, but it appeared she made exceptions every now and then. "It's good to be back. I'm ready to settle in."

Maybe Reese had spent too much time in the city, but everyone listening in on Noah's future plans had her a tad bit uncomfortable. The townsfolk were the same in Heartland, but this was different. It was as if the customers were well aware of the Kendall clan's family issues and were just waiting for the wrong thing to be said. She didn't like it, and she certainly didn't want to be here when the bomb dropped.

"Here you go," Reese whispered, handing Molly a twenty-dollar bill. Her meal and dessert had only come to fifteen dollars, but she always tried to tip well. She'd been a waitress once back in college and understood what a thankless job it could be. "I'll see you tomorrow. I gotta get going while I still got some light."

Calvin had chosen that moment to stand up from the counter, giving Reese the perfect opportunity to talk to him as they both left the diner. There was only one problem. She had to get past Noah and Jimmy to reach the door.

"Excuse me," Reese said softly, having every intention of going around them. Unfortunately, Jimmy backed up with the objective of giving her space. It did no such thing. Instead, she was forced to turn her body as she slipped between the two men. "Sorry."

"It's no trouble at all."

The richness of Noah's tone practically danced over her skin. Their eyes met once more. Was it even possible for a man to have eyes as pretty as he did?

Reese was finally able to breathe somewhat easier when she pushed open the glass door of the diner and stepped out into the sunshine. The humidity of the late afternoon air hadn't diminished in any way, but it was somehow cooler than being in Noah's direct presence.

She would do well to stay away from him, especially considering he was related to Lance Kendall. It wasn't that she thought that any of the teens who had attended the summer camp with Sophia and Emma were involved in their disappearances. After all, twelve months separated their cases.

But ever since Reese had seen the two of them smiling together in that picture she'd found in Sophia's room, she hadn't been able to shake that what happened to the both of them was somehow related. It would be really nice to give her family some closure, if it was at all possible.

"Oh, excuse me," Calvin Arlo said after opening the door behind Reese. She hadn't moved far enough out of the way for him to step out onto the sidewalk. "I didn't see you there."

"I should be the one apologizing," Reese said with a smile, shifting so that he could close the door behind him. He regarded her rather suspiciously as he slipped his John Deere cap over his greying hair. "Actually, do you mind if I walk with you? I was hoping to stop by your store for a…"

Reese continued talking about the weather and how buying some fans to alleviate the heat was her best option since the place she was renting didn't have central air. Calvin went over her options with the items he had in stock, but it was when they finally reached his storefront that he surprised her by calling her bluff.

It appeared she hadn't been as indiscreet with her questioning as she'd thought.

"You know you don't have to buy a fan to get me to talk about Emma," Calvin said rather dryly as he unlocked the door to his hardware store. He then lifted the bill of his cap to get a better look at her. "So tell me, why are you going around town and digging up old memories best left lost and forgotten?"

CHAPTER SIX

NOAH PULLED HIS truck to a stop alongside the curb in front of a familiar vacant storefront. He smiled when he caught sight of the *Sold* sign propped up in the window. The last time he spoke with Gwen, she mentioned she'd signed the papers to buy space next to the First National Bank. It was a premium location for any financial advisor.

The entirety of Gwen's clientele had already been made aware of her intent to relocate to the Midwest. The majority were maintaining their accounts due to her success with making them even more money above and beyond due to her expertise in spotting a specific company that had the capability to become a thriving success.

The data collection side of the business wouldn't be affected by location, nor was her ability to affect timely trades with modern communications equipment. His sister had been able to negotiate a three-way deal between the bank, the town's local Internet Service Provider, and the software providers of her financial business to share access to the only T3 Data/Voice service connection in town.

Noah was looking forward to having his sister come home to stay, and she was certainly in for a surprise just like he'd gotten. Their dad made no mention of which other houses had been acquired. Unfortunately, there were a lot of abandoned properties due to the local economy.

He leaned over the passenger seat to see if there was an overhead sign still hanging to give any indication as to what had most recently gone out of business, thus enabling his sister to acquire the building.

Nothing remained behind.

Noah barely recalled the Farmer's Cooperative being one of the building's original owners back when he was a kid. Mr. Haney had always given them candy from the dish he kept on his desk. Those Werther's Original Caramel hard candies had been his favorite.

A quick glance over his shoulder at the bakery and the meat market had him remembering a video store also being there last time he was here on leave. Even Blyth Lake had caught up with technology. With improved access to the world of commerce, more new businesses would come to town to revive Main Street. The community would have a place to gather once again, allowing the people the ability to breathe just a bit easier and gain some hope for the future.

Speaking of which, he'd have to spend tomorrow morning on the phone getting the basic electrical service and other utilities started up at the old place. It shouldn't be that hard to do considering the electric service panel was still in decent shape. Nearly everything after that point would have to be rewired.

In fact, he was thinking of upgrading the service to one hundred and fifty amps rather than the standard one-hundred amp service to give him the framework to outfit the house to modern specifications. He'd even like to add a panel in the barn.

If he had to strip the place down to the studs, he might as well install network cabling and wiring to support built-in sound systems. Just about every home these days had a network of some sort and internet access. He had the knowledge to do most of the work himself.

The geneses of his building excitement at what the next few months held in regards to his future had him reaching for the handle on the door. He didn't bother to use the running board as he stepped out of his truck.

"Noah Kendall," a female voice called out. "Is that really you in the flesh?"

He suppressed a groan of annoyance at his incredibly bad luck. Whitney Bell had been quite popular back in their high school days, but she'd followed in her father's footsteps when it came to manipulating the people in her life. Jeremy Bell had been nothing but a third-rate grifter. He still was, as a matter of fact.

"Whitney, it's good to see you." Noah bent the truth a bit, but she didn't have to know that. He walked around the front of his truck so she didn't have to come out into the street to greet him. She hadn't been on the sidewalk when he opened his door, so she had to have been using the ATM inside the bank. The lobby closed at five-thirty, but the cash machine in the foyer was always accessible. "I was just talking with your dad over at Tiny's. He mentioned you were back in town."

"Did he also let you know that he's been diagnosed with kidney failure?" Whitney was never one to beat around the bush. Noah leaned down and gave her a hug, patting her on the back in sympathy while purposefully not inhaling her overpowering layer of cheap knockoff perfume. There were times when silence was the best answer. "He shouldn't be drinking."

Noah stepped back and nodded in commiseration. Jeremy Bell wasn't known to take anyone's advice, especially from his nagging daughter.

"I heard he's been through a lot this past year." Noah shifted his weight as he chose his words carefully. "Between losing his factory job, early retirement, and his declining physical health, it can't be easy. Have you consulted with his doctor about—"

"About the fact that my dad's a habitual alcoholic?" Whitney worded the question for him with a tilt of her head. The ringing of her cell phone didn't stop her from answering. "He refuses to go into the city to see the specialist. Doc Finley is the only one he'll see. I expect that will end up killing Dad."

Noah wasn't sure what to say regarding the fact that Dr. Walter Finley was still practicing medicine. The man had to be at least eighty years old by now. He also doubled for the town's vet in a pinch. There was actually a much younger guy with a professional veterinarian's practice in town now, but a lot of the old timers still used Finley.

"I've got to take this," Whitney said with a sigh of mild annoyance. She was already walking down the street as she tossed a goodbye over her shoulder. "I'm sure I'll see you around now that you're back in town."

"Take care, Whitney."

Noah palmed the keys to his truck as he stepped off the curb, thinking he'd just been saved by the bell. He made his way across the street with a quick grin. He couldn't help but look back to make sure that Whitney made it to her car safely, but it appeared she'd walked to the bank from her father's place. The Bells lived on Third Street in a rundown two-story house that could use a fresh coat of paint and had seen much better days by the general look of things.

Whitney seemed on edge, but so would he if his father had been diagnosed with kidney failure all the while refusing to give up the bottle. It was only a matter of time before the man drank himself into an early grave.

Noah sighed with relief upon seeing the neon *Open* sign lit up in the window of Calvin's shop. Blyth Lake Hardware was the name it had opened under more than eighty years ago, and it was highly doubtful that moniker would ever change.

A loud bell overhead clanged to signify a customer had arrived on his doorstep. Calvin was probably getting ready to close, seeing as it was a few minutes after six o'clock. Everyone was well-acquainted with his love of fishing and that he kept different hours than most during fishing season. In this case, it worked out for Noah just fine.

"Calvin? You around?"

"In the back here," Calvin called out, most likely drinking his coffee while restringing one of his various fishing poles.

Noah was starting to feel like a kid in a candy store as he walked down the main aisle to the back room where Calvin still maintained a small black and white television set that he refused to upgrade. He used it mostly for the sound, according to his story. Spending money for a better picture was senseless in his mind, and he'd stated that very fact to anyone who would listen. Some of the businesses in Blyth Lake might have been affected by the arrival of new technology, but that didn't mean that all the residents would succumb to its charms.

"I'm glad you're still here," Noah said before turning the corner. "I was hoping to grab some—"

Noah broke off when he saw that Calvin wasn't alone.

Reese Woodward was curled up with a glass of lemonade in Calvin's favorite leather chair that had seen better days. A couple strands had fallen from her hair clip and were framing her face. The light chestnut color brought out the flecks of gold in her eyes.

"Noah, congratulations on the new property." Calvin greeted him from his roost on an old wooden stool. He shifted his coffee cup to his left hand before extending his other arm. "I would have stuck around the diner to see what tools or supplies you might need, but I didn't want to be the one to spill the beans to your Uncle Jimmy, if you know what I mean."

Noah didn't want to talk about his uncle. He was more curious as to why Reese Woodward was sitting in the back of a hardware store enjoying a glass of lemonade as if she owned the place. She raised a hand and wiggled her fingers in greeting, much like she had when she'd taken the shortcut on his property.

He smiled and leaned against the doorframe after shaking Calvin's hand.

This ought to be good.

"I don't believe we've formally met." Noah wasn't going to wait for Calvin to get around to making introductions. "I'm Noah Kendall, your next-door neighbor of sorts."

"I'm Reese...Reese Woodward. I hope you don't mind I used the shortcut next to your place when I was heading into town," Reese said an infectious smile. Was that a dimple on her right cheek? "I hear a thank you is in order."

For a moment, Noah wasn't quite sure what she was talking about. He was still focused on the little fascinating indentation. He'd always been partial to dimples.

"I'm sorry. For what?"

"For your service," Reese clarified with appreciation, lowering her legs and sitting forward on the edge of the cushion. "Mr. Arlo has been telling me about your family's legacy of service. I think it's very honorable that you and your siblings chose to carry on the tradition."

Noah was never one to take praise for doing what he considered his duty. He welcomed Calvin's interruption.

"Is Gus in front?"

"No, I left him at Tiny's to finish his beer." Noah caught Reese looking at her watch. Seeing as she walked here, it didn't surprise him that she would want to make it back to her house before dark. He'd taken the shortcut she'd used several times back in his day, but he always made sure to have a flashlight. "Chester and Stella's anniversary is coming up. He wanted Dad to make one of those fancy standing jewelry boxes for her. I figured you'd be closing soon, so I wanted to grab some boards so I can cover up some of those broken windows I inherited."

"I have some AC lumber in the ready bins out back that would do just fine." Calvin set down his mug and unhooked what had to be around fifteen keys from his keyring attached to his belt. "Let me bring some up for you."

"Mr. Arlo, I really should be—"

"Call me Calvin, dear." Noah hid a smile when Calvin tipped his cap, proving that his manners hadn't faded with age. "Call me Calvin. And if you have any other questions regarding Emma Irwin, you know where to find me most days except Sunday."

"I appreciate you taking the time to talk to me. Thank you."

Noah had to have heard wrong. Emma Irwin? He hadn't thought of her in years, and this was the second time she'd been brought up in one day.

"Emma Irwin?" Noah asked, confused as to why Reese had questions about Emma. An unsettling feeling hit the pit of his stomach. "Why would you be asking questions about Emma?"

"I'll let Reese explain while I go back and sort out your plywood and some two-by-fours." Calvin waited for Noah to back up out of the way before he slid past and started walking to the locked door no more than twenty feet away. "How many do you figure you'll need?"

"Enough to cover four regular-sized windows. Say…two sheets of plywood and four two-by-fours," Noah replied distractedly, not taking his eyes off Reese. She appeared a bit uncomfortable that Calvin had left her to her own devices. She set down her glass, still half full of lemonade, next to Calvin's coffee cup. "Did you know Emma?"

"Not exactly," Reese hedged, slipping her hands in the back pockets of her denim shorts. It dawned on him that she never had the chance to answer Molly's question he'd overheard at the diner. "At least, not personally. My cousin went to summer camp with Emma a few months before she went missing that fall."

Noah waited to see if Reese would continue her story, but she fell silent and stared at him expectantly. She was waiting for him to move out of her way, but he was too curious now to let her go without answering a few more of his questions.

"I'm sorry, I didn't realize your family was close to the Irwins." Noah tried to recall someone with the last name of Woodward, but the surname wasn't familiar. "Did your cousin go to Blyth Lake High School?"

"No, actually. Sophia and I grew up in Heartland." Reese's gaze shifted past his shoulder, alerting him that Calvin had grabbed the order of lumber. She relaxed somewhat, almost as if she were grateful for the interruption. "I really should be heading back before it gets dark."

"I can give you a lift," Noah offered, the words escaping his mouth before he could catch them. Hadn't he said to himself not four hours ago that it wasn't any of his business why she was in town? Then again, he hadn't known it involved Emma. "I'm driving right past your rental. I'm heading back to board up those windows for the night."

"I appreciate the offer, but I think Molly gave me a bigger piece of apple pie than she did anyone else today," Reese said, declining his offer as she rested a hand over her stomach. "The walk will do me some good."

"Noah, can you grab these while I lock up back here?"

"Sure," Noah replied, reluctant to end his conversation with

Reese. She certainly had his interest piqued. "I was just offering Reese a ride home. She took the shortcut through the woods next to Yoder's property."

"When are you going to stop referring to the farmhouse as someone else's place?" Calvin gave a hearty laugh as he secured the lock on the storage door. "She's all yours now, Kendall."

"That she is," Noah replied with a smile, a deep sense of pride filling his chest at the gift his parents had seen to give him. Gus might say it was all Mary's doing, but Noah had never seen either one of them do something without the other's consent. They had been partners in every sense of the word. "As I was saying, Reese, I'm heading that way. You're more than welcome to ride over there with me."

"I think you missed her," Calvin said just as the bell above the door chimed Reese's departure. He started walking toward the front of the store where the old-fashioned register was still in place from when his grandfather used to run the store. "She's a real sweetheart, that one."

"She seems nice enough." Noah was very careful with his words, not wanting Calvin to take his interest the wrong way. Blyth Lake had a reputation of having the fastest gossip grapevine in the state of Ohio. He didn't want to be feeding the spread of stories just as he got back into town. "What's her interest in Emma Irwin?"

"Oh, that," Calvin brushed it off as if that topic of conversation came up a lot. Maybe it did. Nothing ever happened around here, so things of that nature tended to hover over the area. Noah *had* been gone for twelve years, only visiting when he got leave between deployments or when holidays had allowed. "She's barking up the wrong tree."

"What's that mean?" Noah asked, shifting the boards in his hands so that he could lean them against the counter, using his knees as leverage. He reached into his back pocket for his wallet. "What is it that she's got wrong?"

"The young lady seems to think there's a connection between her cousin and Emma Irwin disappearing."

"Is there?" Noah asked, handing over twenty-five dollars in cash. Calvin never liked the idea of credit card machines. It was all pay by cash or go without. "A connection, I mean?"

"I doubt it." Calvin rang up the purchase before writing it down on the receipt pad. He tore the top sheet off and handed it to Noah. "She didn't seem all that happy with what I had to say. In all honesty, it sounded to me like her cousin ran away from home. The young lady refuses to accept that as the truth, and her hunch isn't paying off. I wouldn't be surprised if Reese Woodward heads out of town by tomorrow morning."

CHAPTER SEVEN

REESE PAUSED THE porch swing with her flip-flop as a third truck came rambling down the narrow lane. She'd first heard the engine of Noah Kendall's F150 around six o'clock this morning through her bedroom screened window. A second vehicle had followed an hour or so later.

Now? It was going on eight o'clock in the morning as dust wafted in the driver's wake of yet another individual who was joining Noah in whatever renovations he'd begun today.

She couldn't hide her surprise as a red Dodge Ram pulled in behind her small Honda Fit on the far side of the house. No one had ever visited her here besides Rose Phifer. The older lady was African American and the wife of Tiny...who happened to be six feet and six inches tall. Together, they owned a few properties in and around Blyth Lake, along with Tiny's Cavern.

Word from the gossip mill yesterday had it that Tiny and Rose had sold off the Cavern to Brynn Mercer. Of course, the topic had changed on a dime the moment Noah Kendall had walked through the diner's door.

"May I help you?" Reese called out after she'd walked to the edge of the porch steps. It certainly wasn't Rose who had come calling. "If you're looking for Noah Kendall, he's at the neighboring property."

"Mornin'." A man around her age, give or take a couple years, stepped out of his vehicle after shutting off his engine. He was tall, lean, and had a charming smile that could sweep most women off their feet. She wasn't immune, but she wasn't interested either. "I'm headed to Noah's place after I take care of that leak in your kitchen faucet."

"How did you know…" Reese let her voice trail off after she answered her own question. She'd mentioned a few things to Calvin last night during their conversation about Emma and Sophia regarding the house. The leak hadn't warranted a call to Rose, but apparently, Calvin had mentioned it to the woman at some point last night after Reese had left him or sometime earlier this morning.

"You've been here a week, right?" The man walked to the bed of his truck and pulled down the tailgate. She was surprised the planks of wood and other material sticking out the back didn't tumble to the ground. "You should know that word travels fast. Calvin spoke to Rose around five o'clock this morning on his way fishing. He mentioned it to her then, along with the fact that he's not so sure you'll be around much longer. Shame. It's always good for business to have tourists other than what the lake draws. Keeps us family shop owners from selling off the homestead."

There were so many things Reese wanted to address in his little speech, but all she could focus on was that Calvin Arlo thought she'd leave after speaking with him last night.

Where on earth did he get that idea?

Calvin had spent a good hour reminiscing about those days when the town would host a summer camp out at the lake with camping and all the other activities that went along with it to give the locals along with the folks from the surrounding areas a place for their kids to spend a week to enjoy themselves during the summer. The program had gone defunct around eight years ago when there weren't enough sponsors to finance the amount of staff required to run the place. The cost for attending the camp had never been enough to pay the overhead. The businesses in town had provided the majority of the support for the camp from the very beginning.

To the best of his collections, Sophia had been outgoing and made friends with everyone, even going so far as to teach Emma how to swim. It was the reason the two of them had become friends. He didn't recall anything unusual that summer.

She didn't have any reason to believe he lied, so why would he think she would leave town? Maybe he figured she'd run out of questions to ask or leads to follow.

"Name's Chad Schaeffer."

Reese moved on autopilot and held out her arm, having already switched hands in order to maintain her hold on the coffee cup. Chad Schaeffer's name was on her list.

"I'm sorry, my mind wandered there for a moment," Reese replied sheepishly, stepping to the side to allow Chad a direct path to the screen door. "My name is Reese, though it sounds as if you already know quite a bit about me and why I'm here."

"Other than you're thirty-one years old, a teacher from Springfield, Illinois who was born in Heartland, Ohio, and renting out this cottage for the summer to find out if Emma's disappearance is linked to your cousin's disappearance eleven years ago?" The laugh lines around Chad's eyes became even more visible as he shot her a look before entering the house. "Nope. Don't know a darn thing."

Reese sighed and followed behind him, wondering what else Calvin had seen fit to share during his run-in with Rose this morning. Although from the sound of it, Chad might have known about her reason for being here long before today. After all, Calvin certainly had.

"It's really not like that," Reese hedged, trailing Chad as he made his way to the kitchen sink. It was apparent he'd been here many times before. "My cousin was Sophia Morton. She and Emma became friends at camp the same year Emma disappeared. Sophia supposedly ran away exactly a year later, but I never believed that. She wouldn't have done that to her family…to me. I thought maybe…"

Chad set his red toolbox down on the faded tile, though he made no move to look at the faucet. There was sorrow and maybe a bit of regret written across his features.

"Okay," Reese conceded, setting her cup down on the table as she took a seat in one of the four chairs. "Maybe it is like that, but I don't want anyone to think I'm dredging up the past to hurt someone or accuse someone of a crime."

"The Irwins no longer live in Blyth Lake, but we were all affected when Emma went missing. It was a bad time for the whole town." Chad gestured toward the coffee maker, causing Reese to feel even worse. She certainly didn't make the best hostess. He grabbed a mug out of the cupboard, not even having to guess as to where the glasses and cups were stored. "Did you know that I was the one who bought the keg and threw that last party at the old Yoder place the night Emma went missing? My dad had delivered some supplies to Pete Anderson earlier that week, so I knew the Anderson family wouldn't be moved in there by that weekend. We weren't going to do any damage or leave a mess, so we thought we could get away with having one more bash before the place was renovated and a family took possession of the property. There isn't a day that goes by that I don't play the *what-if* game. What if I hadn't given her the booze?"

"You were also at the camp, weren't you?" Reese inwardly cringed when her inquiry came out more like an accusation. This was not how she thought she'd spend her morning. "I'm sorry.

That came out sounding wrong."

"It's okay. I figured I was pretty high up on your list of peo-ple to talk to anyway," Chad said somewhat wryly, leaning back against the counter. He had work boots on with a pair of faded and ripped jeans. There was already a grease stain on the front of his t-shirt from an earlier call. He must start work at the crack of dawn. "I was at the camp, and I do remember Sophia. She taught Emma how to swim, which was quite a feat, as I remember it. Not even Emma's sister could coax her into the water. Those two hung out for most of that week, but I don't recall Sophia ever coming back to Blyth Lake at any point."

That's what Calvin Arlo had said, as well. Reese knew that to be true, but she hadn't realized Sophia had grown so close to Emma.

"What do you think happened to Emma?" Reese asked quietly, pushing aside her empathy in her quest for answers. She *needed* answers.

"It really depends on the day, sometimes the time of year, and who I'm talking to at the moment." Chad stared into his coffee as if the magic brew held the key to one of the town's most tragic mysteries. He finally gave up his search and set his gaze on her. "You won't find what you're looking for here, Ms. Woodward. There are a lot of residents in Blyth Lake who would give just about anything to know what happened to Emma. Me included."

Reese thought she knew what she'd hoped to gain from her vacation here, but now she wasn't so sure she found what she wanted. Chad silently got to work, setting his untouched coffee down on the white laminate counter. The clinks and clanks of his tools from underneath the sink gave her time to think about what to say when he was done.

Should she apologize? It was more than apparent she'd

dredged up memories Chad Schaeffer would soon rather forget, but he hadn't been able to even with all the time that had passed. At the same time, she understood what everyone in town had undergone when Emma went missing. The same thing had occurred in Heartland, only with a different girl a year later.

How could it be that she was the only one seeing a connection here?

"Do you think Emma ran away?" Reese asked, unable to leave well enough alone. She stood from her chair at the kitchen table while Chad unfolded his large frame and lifted the lever of the faucet. The water flowed smoothly, but more importantly stopped when the lever was pushed down. "Was she upset with her parents, her sister, or maybe one of her friends?"

"Emma was the most well-adjusted girl in Blyth Lake High." Chad pulled out the rag that he had stuffed in his back pocket before wiping his hands on the somewhat clean material. "No one ever believed she ran away from home, nor did the sheriff ever push that story. There wasn't a resident in Blyth Lake who didn't join the searches, my brothers and I included. We systematically searched the entire town and the surrounding area. Nothing was ever found."

Something else was bothering Reese that she wanted to clear up, or else she might go crazy out here in the country by herself.

"How did you know how old I was?"

Her question elicited a chuckle from Chad as he began to put away his tools.

"You rented a house from Rose and Tiny." Chad didn't have to explain further. Reese nodded in understanding as she recalled the rental form she had to fill out a couple months prior to arriving in town. "Rose uses Harlan Whitmore to do her background checks. Beth Ann Mason is Harlan's secretary, and Beth Ann is dating Molly's son, Jack Stuart."

Reese was actually quite proud of herself that she followed Chad's little gossipmonger corn maze. The only thing that had taken her by surprise was the name of Molly's son.

Jack Stuart. The name was on her list, but she'd never made the connection to the waitress at the diner.

"I guess you're right," Reese conceded with a shrug and a half-smile. "It was pointless of me to try and come here asking questions without being completely upfront with everyone involved."

"You have nothing to be sorry for. You have every right to seek answers." Chad appeared to truly empathize with her position. He closed the cabinet doors below her sink before picking up his metal toolbox. "You're searching for closure because you lost a family member. Don't ever apologize for doing what needs to be done."

Chad lifted the mug of coffee he'd left on the counter and took a heavy draw. He gave her a smile of appreciation as he set the empty cup into the sink after rinsing it out.

"The faucet is good to go, though these old pipes have a way of becoming loose with just a knock or two. Feel free to call me. I'm on Rose's speed dial—twenty-four seven."

"I thought I saw your last name listed in the notes she left, though another first name was written down. Wesley, maybe? Regardless, I didn't want to bother Rose for something so minor."

"Wesley is my brother, but he's moved on to bigger and better ventures." Chad rolled his eyes good-naturedly, apparently thinking differently than his brother. "Speaking of which, I do hope you find some closure here. Emma's family moved away from the area years ago, but there are still townsfolk here who know what you've been through and can relate. Talk to them. Find some peace. It's what we all want."

Reese came very close to giving Chad Schaeffer a hug for his advice, because it was very sound. This little excursion away from her everyday life wouldn't bring Sophia back to her, just as it was doubtful she would find any answers as to what truly happened all those years ago.

"You mentioned you were headed next door?" Reese followed Chad out to the porch. He made his way down the wooden steps. He paused long enough to look at the one plank that she constantly avoided, though he didn't break stride. "Are you the contractor?"

"Contractor?" Chad seemed surprised that she would think he would be the one renovating the house, but she wasn't sure why. His truck read *Schaeffer's Contracting & Flooring.* "Noah Kendall wouldn't have anyone other than his brothers, sister, and him touch that place if it wasn't for the state mandated inspections. I can get him some items on discount, so I'm heading over there to get measurements and fill out the permits."

Chad loaded his toolbox in the bed of his truck and then lifted the gate until it was securely latched. He reached into the front pocket of his jeans and pulled out his keys.

"I'll be back in a day or two to fix that rotted board in your porch and to check over the rest of it. If you have anything else to add to the list, just give me a call." Chad gave her a wink before he slid in behind the steering wheel. The engine came to life as he leaned an elbow out of the open window. "By the way, you might want to talk to Rose. She wasn't listed as a counselor at camp the year Emma went missing, but she was there the whole time. In fact, she was the one who gave Sophia her assistant swim coach badge at the closing ceremonies. Maybe she has some insight on Emma and Sophia that will help you find what you are looking for."

CHAPTER EIGHT

NOAH TILTED THE water bottle and downed the rest of the contents. He'd need to get a kinetic water softener with an ionizer for filtering the water coming from the well.

Since Blyth Lake was on the Great Lakes water table in this region. The sulfur smell when he used the water heater would be overwhelming if he didn't use an ionizer to filter out the heavy metals, iron, and sulfur. He would need the Reverse Osmosis filter for drinking water, too. Otherwise, he'd have to get used to the taste of well water all over again.

It was close to ninety degrees in the sun today, but it wasn't anything near the temperatures he and his unit had to endure during their time in Afghanistan. Ohio was a paradise in comparison. Civilians would never know just how good they had it every day with running water and electricity that was working ninety-nine percent of the time.

Even Europe had rolling blackouts regularly. Third world countries might only have power for a few hours a day, and even then, it was surging in frequency. The available current was impossible to predict. Quite often, when the power was turned back on each day, something would catch fire or the draw would blackout half the city.

Noah wouldn't miss those places, but he would certainly miss bitching about them with his fellow Marines.

"We should break for lunch. They've got a pulled pork

sandwich on a Kaiser roll at the diner on special that will knock your socks off. Oh, and don't forget to get the seasoned fries with it."

Gus used his handy blue handkerchief to wipe his forehead as he walked down the porch steps. Noah had been keeping a close eye on him, not wanting his father to overexert himself. Regardless of what Doc Finley or the Cleveland heart specialists said about him being cleared for light duty, it was always better to be safe than sorry.

"You go ahead." Noah screwed the white cap back on the plastic bottle before throwing it into the large trash can he'd set at the bottom of the porch for scraps. "Would you mind bringing me back a club sandwich with steak fries? I want to stay and finish clearing out the drywall on that false wall and open up the kitchen for a little more light."

"Don't even think of starting on the kitchen cabinets." Gus meticulously folded his handkerchief back up into the standard square and shoved it in the back pocket of his tan nylon work pants. His dad never wore jeans, but instead preferred the Levi khakis that gave him more leeway when working. "Those granite countertops the Andersons had installed need two people to move."

"Don't worry. I won't go near the counters. I think I'll take a sledge hammer to that dividing wall. I can clear a decent path to the kitchen, which will make it easier to remove the counters and maybe I can keep the cabinets that I want for storage downstairs in the basement." Noah heard the rattle of an engine, automatically distinguishing the truck as Miles Schaeffer's beat-up old Chevy. His son stopped by earlier to take measurements for some much-needed supplies, but to also bring some specialty tools for Noah to borrow instead of buying then for one-time usage. It appeared Chad had gotten hung up at another site. "I didn't know Miles was still in the business."

"Miles had no choice after Wes and Clayton started that huge construction company in Cleveland. They got twenty-plus trucks and fourteen full-time crews working." Gus shook his head in disappointment. Family was everything in these parts. "I'll be back in around an hour. Call me if you need me to pick anything up from Calvin's shop before I drive all the way back out here."

"Gus," Miles said as Gus waved in his direction. "Save me a seat at Annie's. I'll be there in around ten minutes, give or take."

"I appreciate you lending me the electric pipe threader and the power bender. Those damn things cost a fortune to buy and the manual ones are a pain in the ass. I'm going to have to run all new natural gas lines, and I'm going to want a generator for storms and such. I wouldn't be surprised if I end up putting a hundred and fifty feet of new half-inch black pipe in this place." Noah walked over to Miles' truck and helped unload the supplies. "I hear you have a pretty big job coming up with the renovations on those two Hanover cottages out by the lake."

"It's a blessing to have the work, that's for sure," Miles grunted as he unloaded a bunch of the schedule forty PVC that Noah wanted for the sewage lines and to vent the water heater. He carried it over to the bottom of the porch and set it on the ground. "Brynn has worked at Tiny's from the moment she was of age. It only seems right to see the Cavern transfer into her hands after all that she's put into it."

"I heard about that while I was at the pub last night," Noah confessed, passing Miles as he transported a couple of new sledge hammers to add to the growing pile. "It's not going to be the same without Tiny."

"Who are you trying to kid?" Miles barked out a laugh as he sidled up to the other side of the pickup's bed. They both grasped an edge of the first of five four-by-eight sheets of blueboard Noah was going to use for the main bathroom. They lowered it so that it was easier to carry over to the porch. "Tiny might be giving up the reins, but everybody in town knows he'll be there every evening keeping an eye on things, as if he still ran the place. He always was protective of that girl."

Noah didn't pretend not to know Miles was talking about Brynn. She'd practically been raised by Rose and Tiny after her parents died. Everyone knew the story and it wasn't pretty.

"So when does your big project start? Chad was saying in the next couple of weeks."

"First week of July," Miles offered up as he stepped away from the pile of supplies. He nodded his approval at what was in front of him before focusing on Noah. "We're doing the renovations for both those cottages already standing, though. Rose thought it would be a good idea to bring in someone else for the construction of the additional outbuildings."

"Let me guess," Noah suppressed a groan, feeling for the man standing in front of him. "Rose reached out to Wes and Clayton for a crew."

"Can't keep her nose out of anyone's business," Miles muttered, giving a dismissive wave toward town. "Busybodies. Every damn one of them."

"You know Rose has good intentions."

"She can have all the good intentions she wants, but it's not going to make me forgive those two bumbling idiots for leaving the family business to start some overgrown handyman company in the city." Miles raised a hand to his forehead and squinted his eyes in the direction of his truck. Noah glanced that way to see what had caught his attention, truly surprised to find Reese Woodward walking up the drive with what appeared to be a pitcher of iced tea held close to her chest and a stack of clear plastic cups. "Looks like you have company, Noah. I best be heading to the diner, or I'll never hear the end of it."

He grimaced when Miles slowly made his way back to his truck. By this time tomorrow, everyone would believe that Noah and Reese were between the sheets. It would appear Calvin was wrong in his assumption that Reese would be leaving town this morning. That alone would make the gossip churn even juicer, because everyone would no doubt believe Noah was heart-torn over the fact that she would be leaving at the end of summer.

Not to mention that every available single woman in town would think that Reese—an outsider from Heartland—was trying to undercut their efforts to snatch up an available bachelor in town. He couldn't imagine what kind of names they'd be calling her at the hair salon twenty minutes after Miles got to the diner.

It was pointless to yell out to the man that Reese's neighborly visit didn't amount to anything as sordid as what was currently running through his mind.

"Ma'am," Miles greeted with a tilt of his hat as he reached up and touched the bill.

"Hello." Reese's smile grew as the decal on the truck caught her attention. "Schaeffer? Are you related to Chad?"

"Yes, ma'am." Miles opened the driver's side door of his truck, patting the side of it in pride. "Chad's my youngest son."

"He fixed the leak in my sink this morning," Reese shared, adjusting the pitcher in her hands.

Noah closed the distance between them and took the plastic carafe from her hands.

"Thanks for the supplies, Miles. I'll get them back to you as soon as possible."

It wasn't long before Noah and Reese were standing side by side in silence as Miles used the circular gravel turnaround to head back into town.

"I didn't mean to disappear on you last night, but I didn't want to rush you," Reese explained, though Noah didn't believe that excuse for a second. He figured it had more to do with Calvin 'fessing up about her real reason for being in town. "I was hoping some sweet iced tea would make up for skipping out on you."

"I'd invite you inside, but…" Noah let his words trail off, but he'd elicited the laugh he'd wanted. "Don't worry about last night. I made sure your lights were on when I drove past last night to board up the broken windows."

"You didn't stay the night here, did you?" Reese looked over his shoulder in what could only be considered unease.

"No, not yet." Noah walked back to the porch, taking a seat on one of the sturdy steps. He made sure to avoid the one that needed replaced. "I'm staying with my dad until I can get the utilities back on and the inside somewhat habitable. I'm done sleeping on floors when it can be avoided. This way, I get a decent bed to sleep on and hot water in the shower."

Reese tucked a loose strand of hair behind her ear as she took a seat beside him, handing over the plastic cups. Her hair was similar in style to how she wore it yesterday, piled high and wild on top of her head. It gave her a carefree appearance, but he could still sense a bit of tension radiating off her shoulders.

A sweet fragrance surrounded him, though it wasn't heavy in the way to suggest perfume. He figured she was using some type of body wash that had a wildflower scent to it, but it suited her. Lavender or lilacs, maybe?

"I've never been this close to the house." Reese gestured behind her and to the left. "The pond out there is massive."

"We used to fish it when I was a kid. Bass and bluegill," Noah shared, recalling memories of when he, his brothers, and his sister would ride their bikes across town. His parents thought they spent time at Blyth Lake, but that wasn't the case. "My sister was the only one of us who ever caught a good-sized bass."

"Is the pond still stocked?"

"I highly doubt it." Noah took two cups and poured them both some iced tea. No matter the reason that brought her to his doorstep, it was still a sweet gesture. "You're more than welcome to try it. Just remember to throw back any bass under a pound."

"Oh, I'm good," Reese protested goodheartedly. She took the cup from his hand. "It must be nice coming home to a house of your own."

"You make it sound like you miss yours," Noah pointed out, lifting the drink to his lips. Damn, but that was fine sweet iced tea. "You said you grew up in Heartland."

"I did, but I live in Springfield, Illinois right now." Reese lifted her flip-flops a step higher so that it was easier for her to rest her elbows on her knees. "I like the independence, but there are times when I miss being close to my family."

Noah would have inquired why she wasn't spending her summer with them, but he didn't have to.

"You can ask me about Lance, you know." Noah figured he'd get to the real reason she dropped by, instead of beating around the bush. "He was at the camp that summer when your cousin was there. I'm not sure what you hope to find other than she learned to swim that season."

"I don't know, either. I made a list of those who attended that year, but I don't think that's going to help me now. It seems that the entire town was involved in that camp in some way or another." Reese sounded so wistful that Noah had to fight the urge to touch her in comfort. She glanced down at her pink toenail polish as if to try and find words. "Chad Schaeffer made me realize this morning that pretty much everyone knows why I'm here in town. It wasn't my intention to stir up a bunch of hard feelings for everyone. I mean, I want answers…but I don't want to upset anyone."

"Not a lot happens here in Blyth Lake," Noah shared, wanting to ease her concerns. He hadn't expected her to look up at him in that moment. Those golden flecks in her eyes had dimmed until they were almost imperceptible. "Residents still leave their front doors unlocked around here. The sheriff deals mostly with domestic calls if someone has too much to drink and making sure Jeremy Bell makes it home from Tiny's. No one was prepared for something like Emma's disappearance."

"Believe me, I understand exactly what you mean."

They sat in silence enjoying the sunshine and the melodies Mother Nature provided. It was odd, considering they didn't know each other. He found her company was soothing.

"I know what you need," Noah said with a smile after five minutes had passed. He set down his cup next to the pitcher and reached for one of the sledge hammers leaning up against the porch. "You need to relieve a little built-up stress."

"Oh, I do, do I?" Reese laughed a bit until she realized he was serious. Her dimple faded, and she raised an eyebrow when he held out his hand. "With a ten-pound sledge hammer?"

"I got an eight, if you'd rather use that. It's amazing what a little physical effort can do to relieve stress." Noah realized his statement could be taken many different ways, though his intentions were truly innocent. Even so, the slight blush that appeared on her cheeks was quite endearing. "Watch that board."

"I would suggest Chad as the person to fix that, but all he did was laugh when I asked if he was the one who was going to be doing renovations for you." Reese stopped before the threshold, almost hesitant to enter. Noah moved the lever on the screen door so that it remained open. "Why are you doing all the work yourself?"

"There's something to be said for constructing one's own home. I guess it was how we were raised with my dad and all." Noah rested his hand on her lower back, the gesture automatic. She instantly moved forward and into the vacant living room. "My dad and I spent the morning cleaning out the trash left behind by the teenagers who were using this place as a party palace. Some things never change, but now that I've got the place, they don't have a choice but to find somewhere else to have their bonfires."

"What is it you plan to have me do with a sledge hammer?" Reese stopped in the middle of the living room and turned around, taking in every nook and cranny of the place. She finally walked over to the banister and ran her hand over the scratched wood. "I didn't realize there was so much potential in here. The floors are going to be amazing once they're refinished."

"I could tell," Noah said with a laugh. He regarded her closely, wondering what it was about the place that made her uneasy. There was only one way to find out. "You haven't seen anyone out here, have you? I know every family who's ever owned this property. They were all good people."

"I'm sorry. There was always something creepy about this place, but now I can see why you bought it." Reese slowly strolled through the small foyer beside the office and the staircase, her fingers caressing the wall. She entered the kitchen and called back, "Look at this view from the kitchen window. It's incredible!"

Noah waited for her to return, her brown eyes now holding that gleam of excitement he'd experienced the moment his father had handed him the key to this place. She frowned when she looked down at the sledge hammer by his side.

"You're not tearing apart this beautiful maple railing, are you?"

"God, no," Noah replied, wondering just what kind of monster she thought he was. "See this wall? It wasn't part of the original design. The Andersons added it on when they bought the place twelve years ago. The kitchen was much more open to the rest of the house."

"You're going to open up the floor plan then." Reese walked back from the way she came, peering inside the small room that wouldn't be there after he was done with it today. "Oh, this is going to be fun."

"Goggles." Noah lifted up the pair his father had brought, handing them to her. "Always wear protection."

Damn. That was the second time his words lent themselves to a slightly awkward sexual innuendo. His words could be taken out of context, although she didn't appear to have done so. He'd been on deployment for way too long to talk with civilians anymore.

"You should take the first swing." Reese lifted the black strap of the clear goggles over her hair and the back of her head. She secured them over her face until the plastic curve rested on the bridge of her nose. "Isn't it good luck or something? This way, you only have yourself to blame if you regret doing the damage."

Noah hadn't heard that particular old wives' tale before, but he wasn't the superstitious type. He handed over the sledge hammer and stepped back, allowing her room to swing the heavy tool.

"She's all yours, honey. Go for it."

Reese bit her lip as she attempted to get a good hold on the rubberized grip over the wooden handle. Once she was comfortable with her grasp, she lifted the heavy weapon and swung for the fences. Her laugh reverberated throughout the empty house as her first try resulted in only a tiny dent.

"You can swing harder than that," Noah encouraged, laughing with her.

Her next strike cracked the drywall.

"You're right," Reese said rather breathlessly with a radiant smile. "This is very therapeutic."

Another blow of the sledgehammer had a piece of drywall falling to the floor, but her swing was off by a half foot or more. The angle of the head had made a rather deep hole.

"You're lucky I don't charge for…" Noah raised a hand to stop Reese from swinging the sledge hammer once more. He stepped closer to the portion of the wall she'd opened without meaning to, wondering what the hell was inside the partition. It looked to be some type of heavy construction plastic wrap. "Wait. Hold up for just a second."

Noah grabbed part of the drywall and pulled it away, hoping to clear whatever was inside out of Reese's way so that she could keep working.

"Noah, is that what I think it is?"

The sledge hammer hit the floor with a thud at the exact moment Noah took a step back at the realization of what was in front of them. Both he and Reese stood side by side as they stared in horror at a secret this house had held for twelve years.

"We need to call the sheriff. Right now."

Noah reached into the front pocket of his jeans and pulled out his phone, blinking one more time in hopes that the grisly scene in front of him disappeared. That wasn't going to happen.

A decomposed skeleton wrapped in plastic stared out from its hiding place inside the wall. The jaw was slightly opened as if to be screaming for help. The color of the hair was still recognizable after all these years.

Just what kind of hideous crime had they uncovered?

Noah and Reese exchanged a horrified glance that conveyed a million words.

They were now bound together after having uncovered a shocking secret someone had wanted to stay buried forever.

CHAPTER NINE

REESE HAD NEVER seen so many different types of law enforcement vehicles in one place at one time, not even when Sophia had gone missing and they had systematically searched the entire county.

There were two local police cars, along with the sheriff's own official vehicle, as well as two state police cruisers and another two state unmarked detective cars parked behind Noah's truck. A forensics van had arrived shortly after the police had pulled in, along with a satellite van with a media crew from Cleveland.

Blyth Lake wasn't nearly big enough to have a local television station. The state police had made them park the TV van with its big tall dish antenna two hundred yards back from Noah's property line. Hell, it was closer to her driveway than his.

As it stood, there was only one light bar still rotating the reds and blues on the sheriff's vehicle. She was pretty sure it was out of habit, because he seemed to want to wash this most recent discovery off his hands and into those who had the proper resources to solve the nature of the crime made obvious by such a discovery.

"...had an inspector come out twice during the time the property was for sale," Harlan Whitmore said to one of the detectives. They were standing beside the forensics van. The real estate agent's eyes were glued to the house. "They never noticed a smell, let alone a body in the wall. Jesus."

There wouldn't have been a smell. Not after all these years. Add in the fact that the body had partially mummified within the plastic trapped inside drywall, it most likely masked any odors the Andersons might have noticed after they'd moved in all those years ago.

Noah and Gus were currently standing on the porch, talking to the sheriff. Miles Schaeffer had followed behind Gus when he'd come from the diner. The forensics team were currently extracting the skeleton from what was left of the wall. A deputy was watching the crime scene crew notate the location of every piece of broken drywall and placing it in evidence bags.

The forensics team were removing the entire wall and bagging the lot.

Another deputy was keeping the media contained to the side of the gravel lane up the road, while a state detective was speaking into his phone and ordering a search of the entire property using ground penetrating radar and divers for the pond.

Reese wouldn't be surprised if more people showed up out of sheer curiosity.

Everyone had to be thinking the same thing—the body that had been hidden inside the walls of the Yoder's farmhouse had to be Emma Irwin. The girl who everyone had known was dead, but had secretly hoped she'd run away.

Reese stood off to the side in the yard, making sure she wasn't in anyone's way. She'd already spoken to the taller homicide detective about how she and Noah had come to find the body. Dusk was falling and hours had passed since she'd set the sledge hammer down and tore off her goggles in disbelief at their grim discovery.

She couldn't bring herself to leave. The forward motion just wouldn't come.

"I heard what happened. Any word on whether or not it's Emma?"

Reese had been so focused on trying to hear what was being said in multiple conversations that she hadn't caught the rumble of additional approaching engines. A quick look told her that more people had arrived as she'd suspected and lined their vehicles along the lane back in the direction of her rental house. They were staying off Noah's property, but only because of the deputy keeping them at bay beside the news crew.

It appeared the townsfolk didn't want to wait to hear something secondhand. This was the biggest discovery in Blyth Lake history.

"Hi, Rose." Reese folded her arms around her waist, wondering how Rose had gotten around the police line. That thought vanished after catching sight of Noah running his hand through his hair in frustration. She wished there was something she could do for him. The police had already told him that it could be at least a couple weeks before they released the crime scene and he was allowed back inside the house. If it were her, she'd have a *For Sale* sign up in the yard by tomorrow morning. "The homicide detectives are saying they won't know anything until they get the…what's left of the body back to their lab."

Reese didn't feel comfortable referring to the person as a skeleton or body. Whoever it might turn out to be had been an actual person, not just a bunch of dried-out tissue and bones.

"It has to be Emma," Rose whispered, shaking her head in sorrow. "She's the only one who went missing in the history of our town. Miles said that the body was found in that extra wall, which the Andersons had put into the house. That poor girl. To be killed and shoved into a wall to be entombed and forgotten for twelve years. No one deserves to be discarded like that. Lord only knows how she died."

Reese had trouble swallowing, wondering if Sophia had suffered the same fate. Honestly, if it *was* revealed that the body was Emma Irwin, then it was possible that Sophia *had* run away or been murdered just like Emma. Had Reese been so blinded back then to whatever Sophia was going through that she refused to accept the truth?

"Your cousin, Sophia, was a nice girl. There isn't anything definite saying she was hurt, too." Rose wrapped an arm around Reese's shoulders and squeezed. The kind gesture reminded her of what Noah had been trying to do. Look at how that turned out. "You should know that Sophia didn't just teach Emma how to swim. She was having a real tough time after losing her grandmother. Sophia was the one to coax her out of her shell and get her to join in on the camp activities. When things calm down here in a day or two, come and talk to me. Maybe I can help you find closure in a way that helps you put this behind you."

A thousand questions whirled in Reese's mind, but she couldn't form any questions. Maybe she didn't want to come off as insensitive to what was taking place directly in front of them.

"Rose, how did you get past Deputy Wallace over there?"

The older, but lovely, woman raised an eyebrow at Sheriff Percy's question. Her hair was cut short, but the grayish black strands somehow came off as stylish with her penchant for wearing silver. The light fragrance of her perfume was a welcome scent from the stale air inside the house.

"This young woman has not one soul in Blyth Lake to comfort her," Rose pointed out, her bracelets creating a melody of sorts as she lowered her arm from Reese's shoulders. "I was going to see that she got home safely."

"Rose, I'm okay," Reese murmured, noticing all eyes in the immediate area had drifted toward them. She patted the older woman's hand. "Really. I'll give you a call if I need anything, as well as take you up on your offer to talk about Sophia."

Rose seemed to believe Reese's declining of the invitation was the sheriff's fault, and the two started nipping at one another. It appeared to be a common event, considering no one paid any attention to them after Reese stepped to the side and made her way toward Noah.

"You doing okay?" Reese wished she could say something that made all this okay. Words wouldn't help. "Is there anything I can do?"

"I won't be handing you a sledge hammer anytime in the near future," Noah said wryly. His tired smile let her know that he was kidding, but she doubted she would ever pick up a tool of any sort and swing it through a wall again. "It appears we attracted quite a crowd."

Reese glanced over her shoulder, seeing a couple more media vans plus a larger crowd than before.

"You know that they're going to think…"

"I know what they think." Noah didn't look too happy when Reese turned back around. This was affecting him more than he was letting on. "Why don't you head on home to salvage what's left of your evening? I have no idea how long I'll be here, but I'm not leaving until most of the authorities and everyone else have vacated the premises. I want to help lock up and secure the house. At least, what they'll let me do."

It dawned on Reese that he automatically assumed either a curious journalist or maybe even a group of teenagers looking for a scare might try and break in to find something of note that they could spread around town.

"Are you sure?" Reese's gaze was drawn to the open front door where a forensics technician was crossing the threshold. "I can stay, if you like."

"I appreciate the offer, but you haven't eaten a thing all day." Noah's name was being called by the technician. "I also appreciate you staying as long as you did, but I've got this covered. I'll touch base with you tomorrow morning."

Noah made his way back toward the porch and then took a couple steps at a time until he was standing next to the forensics tech. The two engaged in a serious conversation, leaving her no choice but to wander toward the police line. She wasn't sure why she was feeling so bereft.

The sheriff had walked Rose back down the lane toward her car, where numerous other vehicles were parked either in the small field or along the lane. The low murmurs of chatter could be heard from the path that would lead Reese back to her place. She wasn't walking straight into that cluster of curious bystanders.

Reese discreetly made her way parallel to the police line back to the other side of the property near the woods, taking a shortcut through the dense vegetation that separated Rose's property from Noah's land. The sun was falling rather fast, but she should be inside before complete darkness descended. Anything was better than facing all the questions that would be hurled her way had she taken the road back.

It was eerily quiet as she broke through the line of the shrubbery. No birds were chirping, no frogs or crickets were singing their evening songs, and the wind had died down so that the leaves hung from their branches in complete stillness.

An image of the skull being revealed flashed through her mind. Emma Irwin's innocent features morphed into the picture Sophia had in her room. Was it really Emma they'd found?

The implications were profound. Wouldn't such a discovery mean that someone within the community of Blyth Lake was responsible for her death? Pete Anderson had been doing his own renovations on the farmhouse twelve years ago prior to moving in, just like Noah was doing now. He hadn't wanted help from Schaeffer's Contracting & Flooring, or anyone else for that matter.

Had Pete Anderson been responsible for killing that poor girl and sealing her body inside the wall?

Reese figured she was halfway to the side of her yard when something or someone moved in her peripheral vision. She stopped and surveyed the area to her right, taking in every tree within her distant field of vision.

Each stood still until one didn't.

Reese covered her mouth with a trembling hand. She didn't know if it was instinctive to keep her presence hidden, or she was just too scared to do anything else.

A dark silhouette stood no more than a hundred yards away looking back toward the direction from which she'd come.

Neither one of them moved.

It took her a moment to realize that the individual was now actually facing her, having known all along of her presence.

Was it a man or a woman?

Reese deduced it was a man from his height and build, but he slowly faded into the shadows before she could make a decision to run back the way she came. She remained still, searching everywhere for which direction he might have taken.

She hadn't realized just how fast her heartrate had accelerated until she tried to swallow. Her carotid arteries were pulsing at a heart-racing pace.

Had the individual simply been someone from the main road searching for a way onto Noah's property? If so, why hadn't he just said so? Or had the man been there all along, watching her progress, waiting for her in the dark?

Reese looked back the way she came, assessing her choices.

She slowly turned in a full circle, wanting to check every angle where someone could sneak up upon her. Little by little, she relaxed until she could force her legs to move in the direction of her house once again.

The clearing finally appeared in front of her, but the sun had set even farther west. She hadn't planned on being gone all day, so she hadn't left the porch light on in anticipation of her return. The glare of headlights approaching from the main road gave some illumination, but that quickly faded as the vehicle passed by to reach its intended destination farther down toward the crime scene.

Reese didn't waste time and quickly jogged across the side of her yard to reach her porch. She took the steps at a rapid pace, almost missing what was out of place before she lunged over the rotted board.

Only there wasn't decayed wood where there had been since she'd arrived over a week ago. At least, she didn't think there was as she stared down at her feet.

Reese unhooked the small key ring she'd clipped to her belt loop on her jean shorts, sliding the key inside the deadbolt. She avoided the area as she leaned forward and slipped her arm inside to flip the light switch.

Instantly, the porch was bathed in a golden hue.

Sure enough, the old board had been replaced with a brand-new plank. All it needed now was a light coat of finish or stain in order to match the others. Chad must have stopped by earlier today, though she was surprised that he hadn't driven over to Noah's when the dirt road had basically turned into a parking lot.

She was appreciative that Chad had fixed the porch, but her previous anxiety had settled in her shoulders.

Had he been the one in the woods earlier?

Her gaze was immediately drawn in that direction, though the light from the porch made it hard for her to see so far out in the darkness. That didn't stop her from dragging her gaze down the edge of the trees. The hairs on the back of her neck tingled.

Someone had been watching her.

Or was it all in her mind?

She did find a body today, and one that had been hidden for many years without fear of discovery. What if that wasn't all that had resurfaced? She had come here to town to stir up long forgotten pain, and while in the process, she'd uncovered someone else's secret.

Distant sounds from next door carried over in a gentle breeze that had finally resumed. An owl began to call for its mate, and a few of the crickets in her yard started to chatter.

Everything was returning to normal, yet she couldn't shake off the impression that it was all a prelude to the coming crash.

Someone was still there out there. He or she had to be wondering why Reese had come here and unlocked their fear of discovery.

Had she just made herself a target?

CHAPTER TEN

NOAH DROVE DOWN the lane, itching to see if anything had happened at his house overnight. The state police had all but told him that he couldn't continue renovations for a couple of weeks until they were sure their forensics team didn't have to revisit the crime scene or resurvey the property.

He understood, but that didn't mean he had to like the delay.

He couldn't help but glance to his left as he drove past Reese's cottage. It was only going on zero seven hundred, so he doubted she'd be awake at this hour on her summer vacation. To him, vacation meant sleeping in until mid-morning, at the very least. He doubted the kind of entertainment he'd provided yesterday was the type she was looking for on her break.

Never had he thought they'd find something so gruesome within the walls of his new home.

The farmhouse came into view, but not before the yellow crime scene banner that the forensics team had strung across his driveway.

Noah pulled his F150 as close to the tape as he could before cutting power to his engine. His father's words came back to him now as scanned the area.

"I'll understand if you want to sell the property."

His dad had asked last night if he wanted to sell the place, but the thought had never entered his mind. He didn't believe in ghosts and wasn't superstitious of this being some kind of bad omen.

This was *his* house. It would become *his* home.

Noah took his time walking around the property, ensuring that nothing was out of place. He didn't stop until he was standing before the front door, the crime scene tape blocking his entrance with the addition of a square self-adhesive warning seal proclaiming the property under the control of the state homicide detectives and any violation of or trespass therein would be considered a felony with severe penalties.

He couldn't remove the strip, so he just checked the dead-bolt.

He was still unwilling to leave until he was sure the inside remained untouched. He was able to look through the one window that had remained intact, immediately noticing the gaping hole where the drywall and the associated studs had been. It was a complete blank, as if nothing of importance had ever been there.

Noah found it hard to explain to his dad, but he didn't look upon the discovery as bad luck or a misfortune that would lead to some type of hardship for him.

No, he was a firm believer in events happening the way they were supposed to in life.

The identity of the body found would hopefully give peace to the family that was left behind.

Everything pointed toward the skeleton belonging to Emma Irwin. Maybe her body being discovered would lead the police to whoever was responsible for her death. He honestly didn't know if it would, considering that was twelve years ago.

It didn't take long for Noah to confirm that no one had broken into the house or even stepped foot on the property, so he finally gave up any thought of gaining entrance and walked back toward his truck. He mentally made a list of additional items he would need when he came back to the house.

He settled in behind the steering wheel of his truck.

He'd place a call into the lead detective this afternoon to see if there were any updates on the case, but he was doubtful they would hear anything on the identity of the body for some time.

It didn't take him long to turn his vehicle around and head back the way he came. He'd almost passed Reese's place when he caught sight of her sitting on the porch with what looked to be a steaming cup of coffee. He turned the wheel and pulled in behind her car before he ever made a conscious decision to do so.

"Morning," Noah called out, shutting the driver's side door behind him. "Is that coffee?"

"It is." Reese had stood from her seat on the porch swing when he'd parked his truck. She was leaning casually against the post and watching his progress as he strolled down her walkway. "Can I get you a cup?"

"I thought you'd never ask."

Noah searched her pretty features before she turned and walked into the house. Her face was bare of any makeup this early in the morning, and he caught the subtle dusting of freckles on her nose. As beautiful as she was, he didn't miss the stress lines around the corner of her eyes.

"Have you heard anything back from the police?"

"No, other than to stay the hell out of my own house." Noah quickly realized that Rose hadn't updated Reese's rental in years. She and Tiny had sunk a lot of money into the cottages by the lake over the years, and now a good portion of their investment would be renovating and adding onto those properties. This cottage was almost a forethought, even being used for visiting family every now and then. "I wanted to make sure no one was foolish enough to try and break into the house to look for some kind of token."

"And?" Reese glanced at him over her shoulder as she reached for a mug out of the cupboard. "Was anything disturbed?"

"Nothing that I could see from the outside. They've got the place sealed up tight as a drum." Noah took the steaming cup from her hand, waiting for her to signal where she'd like to sit down and talk. The faint lavender scent he'd come to associate with her hung lightly in the air. "How are you holding up? I am truly sorry that I ended up dragging you into that whole mess yesterday."

"It wasn't like you knew there was a body inside one of the walls of your recently purchased home." Reese didn't do a good job of suppressing a shiver of revulsion. She gestured toward the small kitchen table. "What are you going to do now? Sell the place?"

Noah figured he'd get a lot of those types of questions, but he was surprised to hear it coming from her. She came from a small town herself.

"I'll wait until I'm given the all clear, and then I'll start where I left off on the renovation." Noah waited for Reese to sit first before pulling his own chair out from underneath the table. He sat down and leaned back against the four spindles. It crossed his mind that his ass might end up on the floor from his weight alone. These chairs didn't look or feel too sturdy. "The house isn't responsible for her death, nor is a body wrapped in plastic going to curse the place somehow."

"So you *do* think it's Emma," Reese whispered, wrapping her fingers tighter around her cup. The warmth of the porcelain didn't seem to stem her shiver. He resisted the urge to rest his hand over hers. "That poor family."

"They'll have closure, at least," Noah pointed out, knowing

all too well what it was like to return from the battlefield having lost a part of his unit. There were times where there was virtually nothing left of their remains to take home to their families. "I'm hoping that whatever the authorities find can lead them to whoever killed her. Twelve years is a long time for a family to wait for justice, but there is always a chance they might find some type of latent print or DNA evidence on the body or the plastic that could give the homicide detectives a lead of some sort."

Noah didn't even want to contemplate what would happen should the body turn out *not* to be Emma Irwin. Her disappearance was the only tragedy this town had truly faced in his lifetime. It was incomprehensible that something even more sinister could have happened twelve years ago.

"So that's it? You're going to keep the house?"

Reese shifted uncomfortably in her chair and tugged the collar of her shirt away from her throat. She was wearing a thin flannel shirt over a white tank top that reminded him of a summer in the '90s. It also reminded him of why she was here in Blyth Lake. He shouldn't even be contemplating the idea that was formulating in his mind.

"Absolutely." Noah answered her question regarding his house...his home. His previous idea came back with a vengeance. "But since it seems I have some time to kill, why don't I take you up to the lake? Have you been up there yet?"

"No, I haven't." Reese swirled the contents of her coffee cup as she carefully weighed his offer. It wasn't until a playful smile crossed her lips and that charming dimple appeared that he realized where she was going with her answer. "The last time I took you up on an offer to relieve some stress, the day ended with the police on your doorstep."

"So today can only be an improvement, right?"

"Oh, my God," Reese laughed, shaking her head as she pushed back her chair and stood. "You're going to jinx us before we even get started."

"Is that a yes?"

"Yes," Reese responded with a smile as she took her coffee over to the sink and poured the remaining dark liquid down the drain. "Let me grab my cell phone. I left it on the charger in the bedroom."

"Bring a bathing suit and a towel," Noah reminded her, having every intention of enjoying the warm weather. Summer passed quickly in these parts. It didn't pay to stand idle too long. "Oh, and some sunscreen or that sun will burn the hide right off you."

Noah sat back and took a drink of his coffee as she left the kitchen. He was unable to keep his gaze from dropping to the seductive sway of her hips. She was graceful in her movements, and he second-guessed his suggestion on how they should spend their day. He'd just returned home after twelve years, and she was only here for her summer break. The way he saw it, they could both use a friend.

On the other hand, a little downtime wasn't a bad thing while he was waiting for the house to be released. There was a lot of work ahead of him that could take months, if not longer. He wasn't normally a dessert before dinner kind of guy, but opportunity waited for no man.

What could it hurt to have a bit of fun?

Noah stood and drained the contents of his mug before placing it beside hers in the sink. He wasn't sure what prompted him to look out the window, but movement near the edge of the tree line was evident.

"Shit," Noah muttered, turning on the heel of his work boot and closing the distance to the front door. He was off the porch and halfway across the side yard before he realized he hadn't told Reese where he was going. He didn't slow down his pace, though. She'd see his truck still in her driveway and know he hadn't gone far. "Hey! Stop!"

He took off at a dead run, entering the thick foliage and heading in the direction of his house. It didn't take a genius to figure out what this guy wanted on the premises.

Noah held up an arm as he ran to ward off the thin branches in his way. One minute turned into two. Six minutes was probably the average time it took to walk between their properties, but he'd managed it in less than three. He wasn't even breathing hard when he came to a stop.

He scanned the house, looking for any sign that the trespasser had entered through the front door. It still appeared secure, as well as the glass pane on the one window and the board on the other.

It didn't take him long to ascertain that the individual must have cut through the shortcut into town. There was no sign of anyone on the grounds, and a quick walk around the edge of the property line confirmed he was now alone.

Who the hell had been wanting a look at the crime scene?

It had to be a reporter or some type of journalist trying to get the scoop on what the police might have found. The brief glimpse of the individual hadn't been enough to distinguish any unique features, but the person had definitely been male based on his build.

Noah pulled out his cell phone and scanned his recent call log, pressing the one he'd dialed earlier this morning. Patty, the sheriff's dispatcher, picked up on the second ring.

"Blyth Lake Sheriff's Office, may I help you?"

"Patty, it's Noah Kendall." He carefully made his way back to Reese's cottage, purposefully drifting his gaze on the ground in case whoever had trespassed had left something behind. "I thought Sheriff Percy was going to have one of his deputies sit on the house for a few days until interest died down. I just chased some guy off my property."

"We're shorthanded today, Noah," Patty responded, her stress coming through the line loud and clear. "Byron Warner called in sick this morning, as did Sam. It looks like that stomach bug got them. Deputy Foster is driving out that way as we speak. I'll let him know what you saw."

The low rumble of an engine broke through the tree line. Noah stepped out of the foliage just in time to catch sight of the deputy's taillights. He wasn't alone. A media van was following close behind, no doubt to record a segment for the noon broadcast.

"Foster just pulled in, along with a news crew." Noah hated the fact that his home had become a fodder for local gossip, but interest would eventually die down. He firmly believed once the identity of the body was revealed, the townsfolk's attention would turn toward Pete Anderson and his family. "You might want to alert the state detectives to that fact, as well."

Patty took the time to say how sorry she was that his homecoming had been tarnished by such a grisly discovery, but he assured her that nothing could take away from his happiness at being home.

"Are you okay?" Reese was leaning her elbows against the porch railing as she tracked his progress across the yard. Her browns eyes had darkened with concern. "What got you so excited?"

"I caught sight of someone heading toward the farmhouse through the tree line." Noah took stock of the light blue bag she had over her shoulder. He'd promised her a day up at the lake. "It looks like it's going to be a popular place for a while."

"Noah, it's okay if you want to stay," Reese said softly, standing to her full height when he joined her on the porch. She'd only put on a light shade of lip gloss, leaving the rest of her features fresh and natural. Her hair was still piled high on her head, causing his attention to shift away from this morning's events. Just how long was her hair? "I was going to head into town anyway to talk with Rose."

Noah considered the alternatives. She'd handed him an opportunity to duck out on a silver platter. Hadn't he been debating with himself on whether or not he'd made a mistake in issuing his invitation in the first place? She was giving him a valid excuse to walk away without penalty.

With everything that was happening at his new place down the road, he considered that what he should do was hang back until things were settled. Then again, fortune favored the bold.

"Did you remember to pack your sunscreen?"

CHAPTER ELEVEN

REESE WAS HOT as a firecracker, and it had nothing to do with the sun beating down on her as she lay on the beach towel she'd unpacked from her bag.

Noah Kendall's gaze generated enough heat that she was surprised she hadn't burst into flames. The sensual warmth had been there from the moment he'd walked into the diner that first day. The temperature only continued to climb with each passing minute.

The happy laughter of children as they ran in and out of the water, the sounds of splashing under bare feet, and the constant hum of conversations surrounding them by beachgoers enjoying the beautiful weather combined with all the other distractions were the reasons she could still breathe.

Here she was, dressed in only a tiny bright red bikini, displaying herself to a man with the tightest body she'd ever seen in person. Her libido cried out in surrender to end her stretch of celibacy she'd had for…well, way too long.

What would her answer be if he asked her out to dinner tonight?

Could she last through the meal without proposing dessert at her place?

Spending the day together in this manner was extremely different than an intimate meal at a fine city restaurant. Various scenarios came to mind on how she could answer without making a fool of herself.

It did dawn on her that she was most likely completely out of her head and fantasizing about something that would never materialize. Noah was trying to make up for yesterday. Friendship was all that was on his mind.

He was currently lying next to her, leaning up on his elbow as he surveyed the collective sunbathers and the swimmers. She noticed that he was constantly on alert for threats without seeming too preoccupied. Was that from his time in the service or was his antenna up because he concerned about the most recent events?

The eerie memory of the man she saw in the woods last night overshadowed her worry about a possible offer of dinner. She honestly hadn't thought about him since Noah had pulled into her driveway this morning. Now, the idea put the brakes on her daydreams.

"Noah, welcome back!"

Noah expressed his appreciation for the greeting, as he'd done numerous times to many of the well-wishers in the last thirty minutes. Several people had gone out of their way already to stop by their small patch of sand to welcome him home, though it was obvious their interest lay more with what he'd discovered in his new house. Each of them had wanted to be introduced to his companion, as if there was no motive to their actions.

Noah was an expert on diverting the conversation, as well as effectively sending them on their way with little more information than they arrived with. These people really knew how to pour ice on a poor girl's promising moment.

The overt female attention he'd received hadn't been much of a surprise. It had finally prompted her to continually remind herself that she'd come to Blyth Lake for a reason. It was true that she was technically here for a vacation, but meeting a man the likes of Noah Kendall hadn't been in the plans.

What was it about him that made her want to get to know him much better?

"Do you see that pier?" Noah asked, causing Reese to snap out of her mixed bag of emotions that had her twisting in the wind. He was pointing toward a distant pier on their side of the lake. She leaned up on her elbows and peered through her dark sunglasses, following his line of sight. "My brother, Lance, thought it would be a great idea to impress the girls by doing a somersault off the end. He must not have tied his swimming trunks tight enough, because they were at least ten feet from where he finally surfaced."

"That's horrible. Did the girls get an eyeful?" Reese joined in his laughter, imagining the scene unfolding in front of her. "Do you and your brothers look alike?"

She thought she was quite successful in keeping the flush from flooding her cheeks. He most likely thought it was from the sun, anyway. She hadn't asked about the resemblance for anything other than helping her think back to a carefree summer that no doubt had included Sophia at one point.

"Pretty much. We all have black hair and blue eyes. We take after Dad, though Gwen looks more like our mother with the higher native cheekbones." Noah lifted his mirrored sunglasses so that they rested on top of his head. Those blue eyes he'd just mentioned zeroed in on her gaze behind her own dark lenses. "You're getting a little red. Are you sure you don't want me to put some sunscreen on you?"

Reese was saved from answering when a pretty blonde interrupted, standing in the sand at the bottom of their towels. This woman only had eyes for one of them.

"Noah, I heard you found Emma Irwin's body. It's just

terrible what happened, and to think she's been here all along."

"The police don't know for sure who it is, and it will proba-bly take a few weeks before they can make a positive identification." Noah sat up and laid an arm over one of his knees. He appeared casual, but she could see it was also his way of protecting his personal space from someone he identified as an intruder. "Whitney, this is Reese Woodward. She's here on vacation. Reese, this is Whitney Bell. We attended high school together."

"You're the woman who was asking around about Emma Irwin before the body was discovered."

Whitney had formed her words into a sentence rather than a question. She wasn't being rude, but then again, she wasn't giving Reese a warm and fuzzy reception either. It was rather amazing, really. Whitney Bell was on her list of attendees that summer with Sophia.

Something held Reese back from asking Whitney any ques-tions, though.

"Reese is originally from Heartland, just up the road a bit. You remember the camp that Birdie used to run here at the lake? Well, Reese's cousin attended one the year before she also went missing." Noah really shouldn't have made the connection, but it *was* the reason he'd brought her up here today. Reese couldn't be mad at him for introducing her to the very same people she expressed an interest in speaking with. There was just something about this woman that set her on edge. "You went to camp that year, didn't you?"

"Who was your cousin?" Whitney asked, taking a seat on the bottom of Noah's towel as if she were going to stay awhile. She wasn't dressed in a swimming suit, but instead wore a pair of short shorts and a white tank top. The skimpy outfit made Reese believe the blonde hadn't yet accepted the idea she'd outgrown her teenage years. "I have a pretty good memory."

"Sophia Morton." Reese reached for her lightweight flannel shirt, slipping her arms inside the short sleeves. She wasn't about to talk about something so important while she was sitting here in a red bikini. She tied the bottom halves of her shirt together, ignoring the material that now stuck to her skin as she rolled the sleeves up to her elbows. "She and Emma formed a friendship that summer, from what I've gathered thus far. I was hoping to find some type of understanding of my own."

"Sophia Morton." Whitney repeated the words as if she were trying to place a face to the name. She even went so far as to rest her finger on her chin. "I think I remember her. She was rather tall and lanky, but had the most beautiful brown hair down to her waist."

Reese's heart ached at the description. A picture of Sophia's radiant smile after getting her braces off materialized as if she were standing in front of them at this very moment.

"Yes," Reese answered after clearing her throat a couple of times. "I've heard that Sophia and Emma became fast friends that summer."

"Emma and I really didn't hang out much," Whitney revealed with a frown, though she waved at someone she recognized walking by them. "I was closer to Shae and a few other girls. Speaking of which, I'm going to have to give her a call after everything that's happened recently. Do you think the police have gotten ahold of Mr. and Mrs. Irwin yet?"

"I'm sure they are waiting on an identification of the body." Noah reached for his t-shirt and drew it over his head to successfully bring this small reunion to a close. He caught his sunglasses before they fell into his lap. He folded them and hooked them to the neck of his shirt. "How is your dad doing today? I heard he had a dialysis treatment this morning."

"He's home resting, but I should be heading back to check on him." Whitney gave Reese the impression she'd rather do anything else than head back home to check on her father. That was unfortunate. She must have a strained relationship with her dad. "I have a friend coming to town who is interested in renting one of the cottages here. Unfortunately, Rose said four of the five cottages are being renovated right now. She's completely booked through the rest of the summer. Any ideas when you'll be heading out of town, Reese?"

"She'll be here as long as she likes, thank you, Whitney. I'm sure you'll figure something else out for your friend," Noah said with a tight smile. "Tell your dad I said hi."

"It was nice meeting you." Reese tried to inject as much truth into those words as she possibly could without sounding disingenuous. Did it make her a bad person to want to retract her statement when Whitney purposefully rested her hand over Noah's and suggested they get together for a drink sometime? "I hope your father feels better."

"Sorry about that," Noah muttered, not bothering to watch Whitney walk away. His attention was solely on Reese. "Whitney is...well, let's just say she's a malcontented character."

"The two of you were involved in high school, unless I'm mistaken. Weren't you?" Reese guessed with a smile, relaxing somewhat now that it was just the two of them. She'd learned days ago that asking questions about Emma and what had happened wasn't the best way to make new friends. "Prom King and Queen, maybe?"

"Lord, help me. You're a physic, too." Noah flashed a smile her way, but it was the crinkles around his eyes that were a dead giveaway that she'd gotten at least part of summation right. "I might have gotten to second base with her in our sophomore year, but she had her sights set on Billy Stanton by our senior year. I was nothing but dust in her rearview mirror by then."

Reese didn't even have time to flinch when a Frisbee came sailing through the air, straight for her head. Noah reached up and knocked it onto a new course before she could react. His quick thinking had kept her from getting a black eye at the minimum.

"Heads up!" Noah called out before turning his head to track down the errant player. A father who was playing with his young son were the guilty duo. It was easy to recognize the wordless exchange between the hapless father and Noah, as they both quickly dismissed the near miss as unintentional. "We've only been here for a half hour, but I'm getting rather hungry. What about you? Could you eat?"

Reese had ridden with Noah in his truck, but that meant stopping by his dad's house for him to grab a change clothes. He'd donned a pair of black swimming trunks with a basic white t-shirt, exchanging his work boots for a pair of leather flip-flops. She'd had to do a double take when he'd walked into the kitchen. There was a lighter air about him that was very fetching.

He'd taken the time to show her around the house, including his dad's workshop and the surrounding property.

To say she was impressed by the furniture displayed in his childhood home was an understatement. The beautiful pieces were handcrafted and the precision in the smallest details was astounding. It was no wonder Noah wanted to renovate his crumbling home on his own.

"I could definitely go for something to eat." Reese glanced over her shoulder to see how long the line was to the concession stand set up on a grassy knoll with a deck overlooking the water. "We could leave our towels here and walk on up to the—"

A man with a ball cap leaning on the wooden railing caught her eye. His expression was hidden behind a pair of black sunglasses. She'd never seen him before, but she could have sworn he was staring directly at her. His gaze unlocked the faintest shiver of fear, similar to that which she'd experienced last night.

"...what is it?" Noah had finally caught her attention. She glanced at him to find him switching his gaze from her to the small concession area. "Reese?"

"That man over there," Reese began as she looked back over her shoulder to point him out. He had disappeared as quickly as she had noticed him. She scanned the people, looking beyond the beach and out into the car lot, but she was unable to spot him. "He's gone."

"Who's gone?" Noah used his hand to push himself off his towel into a standing position. He shielded the sun with his hand and skimmed over the occupants coming and going. "What did you see?"

"Nothing, really." Reese brushed off his concern, feeling somewhat embarrassed that she was this jumpy over someone who'd done nothing wrong. She wasn't even sure he'd been looking at her, and that certainly didn't constitute a crime anyhow. "I'm just a little jumpy after yesterday."

"Understood." Noah offered her a hand, helping her stand. He took her by surprise and stole her breath when he didn't release her right away. He lifted her dark sunglasses and set them gently on top of her head. He gazed deep into her eyes from no more than six inches away and said, "I *am* sorry about yesterday. And today. I know Whitney made things uncomfortable with the way she handled my inquiry on your behalf."

"You're not responsible for Whitney or anyone else in this town, for that matter." Reese didn't like that he could read her so easily or swing her emotions quite so readily. She thought she'd hidden her discomfort rather well. "I came here asking questions about Emma. Now, I'm half-responsible for the hidden body of a possible murder victim being discovered after twelve years. I'm sure I'm not the most popular tourist in Blyth Lake at the moment."

"You forget I'm the party responsible for the second half of that equation," Noah said wryly, finally allowing her fingers to slowly slip from his. Her skin still retained the heat of his touch. "Come on. Let's see if we can't find Rose and get some of your questions answered. Besides, we're attracting the attention of the entire population of Blyth Lake."

Reese quickly stepped into her jean shorts, buttoning them over the bottom half of her bikini. She then grabbed her tote and picked up her flip-flops. She found herself scanning the people in line, those coming in from the beach, and the surrounding tables for the man she'd seen just a few minutes ago, but he was nowhere to be found.

The light touch of Noah's hand on her lower back chased away all the stress that had settled in her muscles. It was as if her ears popped after a long flight in midair. Children's laughter rang out as they splashed in the water, the bright sun continued to warm the sand, and today was meant to be enjoyed by even the most ill-fated summer vacationer.

Reese couldn't help but wonder what the night might hold for them both.

CHAPTER TWELVE

NOAH TIPPED UP his glass of sweet iced tea and drained the last of its contents as he listened to Rose reminisce about the past. They'd all eaten lunch together, allowing Reese to ask the older woman all the questions she'd thought to examine since arriving in Blyth Lake. Technically, ever since she'd found the picture of her cousin and Emma Irwin together taken at the camp.

Rose had been Birdie's protégé and had eventually taken over what was left of the business here at the lake after the older woman had passed on from what the townsfolk believed to be a broken heart. Her husband's death had left a hole in her that she'd never been able to fill. The same could be said for both of their absences now that they'd left behind a legacy that would be fondly remembered for an entire generation of children.

"Those camps were good for the kids. I was sad to see them end, but Birdie had been adamant that she couldn't run another one without her husband at the helm." Rose used one of her new brochures to fan herself. Not even the shade of the umbrella above the table helped with the heat. "I almost started back up the tradition around five years ago, but Tiny and I never seemed to have the time to organize it."

"Sophia always came back happier after spending a week or two here," Reese said as her phone chimed once again. It was the third time she'd ignored whoever was calling. "Her brother,

Tanner, was at the camp that year. He recalled Emma, but he was pretty sure she and Sophia didn't keep in touch after those weeks were over."

"That's not too unusual. Friendships are made and then everyone goes back to their own lives." Rose switched the fan to her other hand without interruption. "As for your Sophia, she and Emma bonded as tight as twin sisters. It wasn't four months later that Emma went missing."

"Lance was at that camp," Noah offered up, thinking back to that difficult summer. "He was also with me at the bonfire the night Emma disappeared. I can always give him a call for you, see if he has anything to add. Maybe some detail he had forgotten about would be key now that we can assume she never left town."

"It's okay," Reese said softly, looking down at the napkin still in her hand from lunch. There was a sadness in her movements that made him want to take her in his arms. "I don't think there's much more that anyone can add. I've been chasing a ghost, and it's time I let her rest."

Noah understood how hard it was to let someone go, whether that person was a friend or family. It could sometimes take years to accept the way the past had played out.

"I understand if you want to cancel your rental agreement for the summer. You should head off to some Caribbean island and drink those famous umbrella drinks everyone is always chatting online about. Not that I don't think our cocktail drinks couldn't rivals theirs," Rose said with a laugh. "Tiny spent a lot of time creating new concoctions for the evening crowd. But seriously, we won't charge you the cancellation fee should you decide to head back home."

"I appreciate that, Rose." Reese pushed back her chair and laid her napkin on the table. She hugged the older woman in appreciation for her time. "Thank you for talking with me, and I'll let you know what I decide. I know you have a line forming for the place."

Noah wasn't going to deny wanting to know her thoughts on leaving, as well. There was something very refreshing about her company that he wasn't ready to have end so abruptly.

"I'm sorry you didn't find the answers you were looking for when you got here." Noah set his empty glass on the table as Reese reclaimed her seat. He didn't ask the question that was on his mind, but he did lead the conversation in that direction. "Out of curiosity, what connection did you think they had?"

"You're going to think I'm crazy." Reese scrunched her nose and then leaned forward, setting her elbows on the table. She lowered her voice so that the nearby patrons couldn't hear what she had to say. "I've had thoughts of a possible serial killer, to someone murdering them for something they might have seen together here at camp, and even them planning to go off to California to become actresses together. Sophia mentioned the latter a time or two, but apparently, Emma wanted to be a veterinarian."

"She did, as a matter of fact," Noah confirmed, thinking back to something Shae Irwin said once about her baby sister. "Emma loved horses. She used to go riding out on Dixon's farm back then."

"Dixon?"

"Raymond Dixon." Noah figured it wasn't easy keeping up with all the families in and around the town of Blyth Lake. "Birdie and Stanley's son. He's the one who sold Rose and Tiny the property surrounding the east side of the lake after his mom passed."

"So that's it, huh?" Reese's shoulders hunched a bit at the realization her quest had come to an end. She rested a hand on her forehead as if contemplating her next move. "I created a fantasy world out of nothing."

"It wasn't in vain," Noah pointed out, wishing he could do say or do something to make her feel better. He made a feeble attempt. "You heard some amazing stories about Sophia that you didn't know before regarding her compassionate nature toward Emma. It sounds like your cousin was very sweet."

"She was, and I think that's what hurts the most. I don't believe she would ever have left her family of her own free will." Reese sat back and laced her fingers together over her stomach. She finally raised her gaze to his as she struggled with acceptance. "It's the not knowing that's the hardest. Why would she up and leave without telling anyone where she was going?"

"That's true, so that's why I think it might be a good thing for you to stick around for a few more weeks. Relax awhile and get to know your neighbor a little better." This kind of knee-jerk blurting of whatever came into his head was becoming a bad habit recently. Noah usually didn't say things before thinking them through. "The Irwins suffered the same thing you and your family did when Sophia went missing. We might have inadvertently given them some closure as to what happened. If that's the case, you had a hand in helping with that."

"Is it closure, though?" Reese leaned forward once more after realizing an older gentleman next to her was looking their way. "If the body turns out to be Emma, that means someone killed her or at least had a hand in whatever ended up killing her."

"Yes, it does," Noah said grimly, reaching for his sunglasses. They really shouldn't be having this conversation out in the open. "How are you doing today, Tobias?"

The older gentleman feigned surprise that Noah had been sitting at the next table all this time without recognizing him. He gave a wave in greeting before opening the book that had been sitting next to his melting strawberry sundae.

"Are you ready to head back to our towels yet?" Noah stood behind Reese and pulled her chair out so that she had the additional room to pick up her tote. "We still have the rest of the afternoon to relax."

Noah wasn't so sure his words rang true, considering they'd been interrupted more times than he'd had a chance to really get to know her.

"Let me stop at the restroom before we walk down to the beach," Reese said, adjusting the straps of her bag over her shoulder. She tilted her head back and truly smiled, giving him hope that this afternoon wasn't a total waste. "I won't be long."

Noah had paid their tab when the waitress cleared their table, so he made his way to the side of the deck to wait near the wooden stairs that led down to the sand. He slipped his sunglasses on as he stepped out from beneath the shade.

Something Rose had said earlier stuck in his head, and he wondered if he couldn't talk Reese into going with him to Tiny's Cavern tonight. Granted, Tiny didn't own the bar anymore, but tradition was a big part of Blyth Lake. Slated on the agenda was the annual dart competition. It got fairly competitive, especially considering Billy Stanton stole the championship title from Chad Schaeffer the last time Noah had been in town.

"Help! Someone call Sheriff Percy!"

Noah immediately reacted, stepping forward before anyone could get in his way. The plea had come from the back where the restrooms were located. His stomach tightened that something might have happened to Reese, but he mentally understood the likelihood of that was next to nil.

"Mindy, what happened?"

Several people already had their cell phones to their ears. He didn't worry that a call wouldn't be placed, but he could offer what help he could before the sheriff arrived.

"That woman you were with just a minute ago," Mindy said somewhat breathlessly, instantly turning and leading him back the way she'd come from. "She was attacked. She's still in the restroom, Noah. She's trying to stop the bleeding."

REESE HELD THE wadded-up paper towels against the side of her forehead, afraid to remove them for fear of bleeding all over the table. The cut she sustained when her head hit the tiled wall of the restroom was pretty bad. She also didn't want to show Noah how severe the tremors were in her hands. He was already upset by what happened, and she didn't want to make the situation worse.

Technically, it couldn't get much worse.

"Are you sure you heard him right?" Sheriff Percy asked, jotting something down in the small notebook he'd pulled from the breast pocket of his uniform. "Maybe you—"

"Sheriff, she's told you the same turn of events three times now."

While Noah berated the sheriff for asking her the same question over and over again, Reese tried to recall anything that would help the man find her attacker. She easily recalled walking into the single stall restroom, but something had prevented the door from being shut. The next thing she remembered was stumbling backward as someone burst in, but she'd immediately put her arm up for protection as the door swung open with a bang.

The man had shoved her hard enough that she'd hit the side of her forehead against the ceramic tile. The stun of the impact had given him enough time to push her face forward against the wall, issuing a warning she'd never forget.

"Leave town, bitch."

"Reese, the medics are here," Noah gently told her, bringing her back to the present. Rose had cleared a section of the tables so that Reese had some breathing room. That hadn't stopped the patrons and beachgoers from watching her from afar, especially once the sheriff had arrived. "They're going to want to—"

"No stitches." Reese was adamant about the no stitches thing. She had a fear of needles, and just the thought of them sticking one in the cut on her forehead made her nauseous. "I'm serious."

"How about you let them look at it, and they can tell you what you need once they see what they're dealing with," Noah suggested in a soothing and calm tone. She didn't want to tell him that his blue eyes had turned to ice the moment he'd seen all the blood in the sink. "I know one of the paramedics. Her name is Julie Brigham. Lance went to high school with her, but she was far too smart to fall for him."

Reese understood that Noah was trying to make her smile, but those three words still resonated in her head in time with the throbbing that had set in upon impact with the wall.

Why the warning?

Why would someone care when or if she left town?

"I-I saw someone in the woods last night. It was when I left your place and walked around the police line into the woods." Reese hadn't meant to take Noah by surprise, nor had it been her intention to keep information from the police. "I honestly didn't think anything of it at the time. Well, I mean, I did then. I was scared at first, but the man was there one minute and gone the next."

"You didn't think it might be worth mentioning after I chased someone away from your house this morning? What about that idiot from earlier? Was it the same guy?" Noah had every right to be frustrated at her omission, but he clarified both of their statements to the sheriff. "I saw someone on the edge of her property line in the woods this morning. I assumed his interest was in what happened yesterday, but he could have very well been there watching for Reese."

"So at three different times someone has either been watching you or tried to threaten you, succeeding on the third attempt." Sheriff Percy finished writing in his little notepad before flipping the cover back in place. He hadn't bothered putting on the hat he'd worn yesterday. "It seems as if you stirred up something with your questions about those girls, Ms. Woodward."

"Sheriff, I've been patient." Noah maintained a hand on Reese's shoulder as he stood to his full height. Regardless that he was still wearing his swimming trunks and t-shirt, his demeanor spoke volumes over the lack of professionalism the sheriff was depicting. "Ms. Woodward has done nothing wrong. She is the victim here. She was attacked in the restroom of an establishment in your jurisdiction. You need to do your job."

"Coming through," Julie called out, edging her way in between one of the deputies and Mindy. Rose had put her hand on the girl's shoulder to prompt her to move quickly. "Noah, good to see you."

"You, too, Julie." Noah didn't bother to sit back down, though he did move behind Reese. She had yet to pull the paper towels off her wound. "Reese hit her head against the tile in the restroom when she was attacked."

"Hi, Reese." Julie already had on blue latex gloves and immediately kneeled before Reese, taking over the pressure she'd been putting on the cut. "My name is Julie. Can you tell me what happened in your *own* words?"

Reese understood it was standard procedure, but she didn't want to go through it a fourth time. She took an unsteady breath and recounted second by second from the moment she walked to the restroom to when Mindy found her leaning over the sink. Noah probably didn't even realize that his fingers became tighter on her shoulder with each word she spoke.

"And before you tell me I need stitches, I'm not getting them. I saw a medical show on television where the doctors can now use glue and strips to close a wound." Reese winced when Julie pressed lightly around her injury. With all her talking, she hadn't realized she'd lowered her hand or that Julie had removed the paper towels. "You have that stuff, right?"

"Not quite, but I think we can work within the parameters of your request," Julie said in appeasement, looking over her shoulder at her partner. "Billy?"

Reese wasn't sure why Julie had called her partner's name until he joined them, prepping the antiseptic wipes and tearing some white backing off what looked like strips of tape.

"Billy and I went to school with Noah. Did you know that…" Julie continued to attend Reese's injury all the while telling a story about the time Billy filled Lance's locker with whipped cream out of a dozen spray cans, only to find out the locker had been Noah's all along. It wasn't long before Julie was asking that Reese follow the beam of a pen light with her eyes. "I've put a butterfly bandage on your wound along with a few steri-strips. There's no sign of a concussion, but should you experience nausea or…"

Julie continued to list symptoms which Reese was now actually experiencing, but not because of her injury. She was nauseous at the fact that someone would go to such extreme lengths to get her to leave town.

Honestly, all today had done was make her believe that

someone had knowledge of what happened to Sophia, as well as Emma.

She wasn't leaving Blyth Lake, not unless this bastard suddenly set himself on fire…and even then, she would take her time.

"I'll keep an eye on her." Noah stepped forward and gave Julie a hug before shaking Billy's hand. "I'm sorry we met back up under these circumstances. I'm sure I'll see you at the Cavern sometime next week."

Reese had noticed the sheriff stepping to the side to speak with his deputy when the paramedics had settled in to attend to her. His lips were set in a thin line as he compressed his lips in annoyance. Two days of activity in his town wasn't improving his mood, and she'd been at the heart of both instances.

"Thank you," Reese said with a small smile, not wanting Julie or Billy to catch on that she had one massive headache. She'd take some acetaminophen when she got the chance. "Noah, I think I'm ready to go home now."

"Sheriff, is there anything else you need from us before you start conducting your investigation?"

Noah spoke to the sheriff about putting a deputy outside her house before getting denied because one was already stationed a hundred yards farther down the road.

Noah then made the case that access to both sites could be controlled from in front of Reese's rental. The sheriff finally relented.

Reese couldn't help but scan the area for the man she saw earlier. She had no doubt now that he *had* been watching her from the boardwalk.

Why?

Noah would probably tell her that it had nothing to do with Sophia and everything to do with Emma Irwin. Should the DNA results confirm the body was Emma, that would mean whoever killed her was terrified the police could now make a connection. But that still didn't explain why someone would come after her. The body had already been found.

"Let's go," Noah murmured, leaning down and picking up her tote that she'd set down beside the chair. He held her hand as she stood from her seat, his blue eyes watching her intently. She did her best not to wince as her head throbbed in time with her heartbeat. "We'll get you settled in at home before we come up with a plan."

Plan? Reese would have asked what he meant by that had Rose not stepped in front of them to see if she could do anything for her. Noah eventually maneuvered her away from all the attention and continued to guide her through the parked vehicles. By then, she was distracted by the throbbing headache she'd been expecting to get worse all along.

The sun continued to beat down on the blacktop. Heat simmered up and licked the sensitive skin on her feet and legs. Her head continued to pound with each step they took, but none of those things compared to the sliver of fear embedded inside her chest because the door was unlocked.

She'd exposed something sinister with that sledge hammer. Whoever was trying to chase her away had probably been the one who killed Emma…and possibly Sophia.

What if she was next?

CHAPTER THIRTEEN

"**M**AYBE YOU SHOULD bring her home."

"I think Reese is more comfortable here, Dad." Noah checked the lock on the back door in the laundry room. Every door in the house was secure, but that left the screened windows as a viable point of entry. Without air conditioning, closing the windows was going to be a problem. "I'll be home sometime tomorrow. We stopped by the house while you were at the diner earlier. I grabbed a change of clothes, my .45, and a box of cartridges."

Noah walked past the small bathroom off the kitchen, back-stepping once he noticed the small window above the toilet. That minor opening would make no different to the heat level in the house, so he shut it tight and flipped the latch. It would be one less entry point he'd have to worry about.

"The town's board members haven't been real happy with Percy lately." Gus should know the opinions of the sheriff, especially given that Noah's dad was a member of the township board. "He's been handing off a number of investigations to the state police that should have fallen under his jurisdiction just to get out of doing the work."

"Why would the state even take those damn cases? The county gets state funds to pay for a sheriff's salary." Noah switched his cell phone back to his right hand as he walked into the kitchen. The curtains were blowing slightly in the warm breeze. The rain that was supposed to hit last night pushed off to the north, leaving behind it a belt of relatively high humidity. "I'm surprised they didn't push them back on the sheriff and tell him to do his job."

"Oh, he's got some buddies up there that owe him some favors, I figure," Gus informed Noah, the disdain for what had been occurring lately evident in his tone. "I reckon they ought to be running out soon. Did you know the election is next year? Maybe you should think about running for county sheriff."

"Me?" Noah laughed as he turned off the overhead light, leaving the lone bulb lit over the sink. "That's more Mitch's thing, Dad. Seriously, you should let him know the election is coming up so he can throw his hat in the ring. He might actually win the election with his background in the CID."

His older brother's picture was next to the word *square* in the dictionary. He had joined the Marines as an MP and worked his way up as a Criminal Investigator. There were other adjectives that came to mind regarding Mitch, but Noah let them slide as he ended the phone call with his dad and rejoined Reese in the living room.

She'd been quiet since their time up at the lake, which was understandable. He hadn't let her see the rage that had invaded him upon witnessing her leaning over the sink as blood dripped down the white porcelain and into the drain. It had never even entered his mind that someone might blame her for the body being discovered in his house. The fact that she had been asking questions about her cousin and her friendship with Emma was circumstantial.

"How's the headache?"

"Same, but I'm more worried about how you're going to feel come morning sleeping on that old couch." Reese gave the old overstuffed sofa a sideways look from her location centered in the front door. Noah refrained from telling her she shouldn't make herself such a targeted silhouetted in the doorframe, but he didn't want to add to her worries. "I'm really okay here by myself. The deputy has driven past three times in the last ten minutes. I can't imagine the amount of fuel he's wasting driving up and down the dirt road like an idiot."

"Don't worry about Deputy Wallace. He's harmless." Noah wanted more than anything to recommend they go back to his dad's house, but all she would do was say it wasn't necessary. This was the only other alternative, because he wasn't leaving her alone out here where she was unprotected. He could also see that she was itching to go outside. "Come on. Let's go sit on the porch for a bit."

Reese reacted faster than he would have thought with that headache blasting away at her temples. She was out the door and sitting on the porch swing before he even stepped over the threshold. He didn't like to see her so defensive and helpless as she folded her arms across her middle before glancing to the left, but she still had the courage to stay in the open.

The edge of the tree line was dark with the occasional lightning bugs coming out to play. The frogs were deep in conversation and the crickets were dancing in the grass. The wildlife would sense a predator in their midst, alerting him to any danger should someone try to approach the porch in the dark.

Had the man who attacked Reese wanted her dead, he could have easily made that happen today with little more than a pocket knife. Whoever it was only wanted to scare her, which challenged his identity as being the same individual who took the time to hide a body in the wall of a home. That didn't mean her attacker wouldn't escalate his intentions at some point if he felt threatened.

Right now, the best thing Noah could do was watch over her

until either the sheriff did his job and investigated likely perpetrators or Reese decided to leave town. He wasn't quite ready for the latter to happen, so he was banking on pushing the sheriff to do what he was being paid to do.

"Spit it out," Noah urged, nudging her with his shoulder as he joined her on the wooden swing. The chains strained from the hook in the ceiling above, but he was used to that with his solid frame. He doubted he'd have this physique in ten years, but he'd take advantage of his strength should it be needed now. No one would have a chance to hurt her while she was here for the remainder of her stay. "What are you thinking?"

Reese sighed in resignation as she lifted her legs and set her bare feet on the edge of the seat, allowing him to be the one to keep them in motion. She wrapped her arms around her legs and rested her chin on her knees as she watched the deputy make his way back down the lane on yet another lap. The faint scent of lavender chased away the damp odor of humidity.

"He didn't say anything other than to warn me to leave town." Reese paused as she visualized what had taken place this afternoon. "But it was as if he wanted to say more when he was holding me against the tiled wall, almost like he wanted to order me not to ask any more questions."

Noah didn't reply, figuring she needed to sort this out herself. She thought her attack had to do with Sophia, but the chances were better that it was Emma's discovery that prompted the assault. Noah fully believed it had everything to do with the incident at the house, but Reese needed to reach that conclusion on her own.

Noah recalled that Emma's disappearance had a lot of townsfolk looking at one another suspiciously twelve years ago. The blame game had certainly made the rounds. His family hadn't been immune to the mob's accusations either. It hadn't been a pleasant time, and he didn't think the situation had changed all that much. The only exception was that the Irwins weren't around to watch their lives disintegrate into nothing but ash like they had twelve years ago.

"He ran out of time, because the place was crowded. At least, that's why I think he didn't say anything else." Reese tilted her head so that she could see Noah instead of the deputy's car that had made a one-eighty at the end of the lane just past his house. Wallace was making his way back. The crunch of the gravel and dirt echoed through the darkness of the night. "That girl, Mindy, she said she didn't see anyone coming out of the restroom. But what if it's someone everyone knows? What if it's someone I've already talked to during the last week?"

"Did you recognize his voice at all?"

"No," Reese replied, frowning before wincing as the cut on her forehead most likely pulled against her hairline. She pressed her fingers gently above the butterfly stitch. "I don't think so, but I've spoken to so many people in town. I don't know everyone, of course, but no one sticks out. He had an edge to his voice, as if he was half-crazy. I tried to be indiscreet in asking about Emma and Sophia this past week."

"Any mention of Emma would immediately set everyone on edge in this town," Noah warned a little too late. He didn't have to tell her that she would have been better off just mentioning Sophia. That point had been proven today. "You're suggesting that Mindy might have seen who it was and decided to protect him rather than say anything?"

"Am I totally off base?"

Noah considered her theory, but highly doubted Mindy would have done such a thing after seeing how hurt Reese had been afterward. Plus, the girl was quite rattled herself. If she had seen the perp, the only thing he could think of that might keep her from saying so was family loyalty.

"You said Mindy came in the door maybe thirty to sixty seconds after you were attacked." Noah envisioned the layout of the short hallway where the men's and women's restrooms were located. He clenched his hand into a tight fist, realizing now what everyone had missed in the immediate aftermath. Damn it. "Whoever attacked you could have easily been able to slip into the men's room without being seen. The doors are literally directly opposite of one another."

Both of them fell into silence. Reese readjusted so she could watch the lightning bugs begin their mating ritual. Noah continued to use his work boot to keep the swing in motion. He'd changed earlier, a hell of a lot more comfortable in a pair of jeans and boots. Should he need to go traipsing through the woods again, at least he'd be prepared this time with a ready firearm for good measure.

"I bet this isn't what you expected to come home to," Reese whispered, reaching up and removing the band she'd used to hold her hair in place. The caramel highlights appeared more golden in the porch light, but that wasn't what took him by surprise. The length of her strands fell around her, almost creating a shield as the waves covered her left arm all the way to her elbow. His fingers itched to see if her hair was as soft as it looked. "I'm sorry that it seems to be me who's got the streak of bad luck lately."

"You might have given a family closure, as well as drawn out someone who might be involved in a murder." Talking about homicide had a way of putting things into perspective. Noah was only here to make sure she was safe. After all, he was partly to blame for the body being discovered. He never should have had her take a sledgehammer to his wall. "As long as the sheriff does his job or maybe the state investigators, you might very well have helped solve a twelve-year-old crime."

"You're a *glass is half full* type of guy, aren't you?"

"That I am," Noah confessed, having spent way too much time in places where there weren't any flushing toilets or running water. "We should be grateful for what we have, and not complain about the things we can't change."

"Are your brothers and sister like that too?"

"Hell, no," Noah laughed, thinking of Mitch in particular. "Wait. I take that back. Lance and Jace don't complain too much. Mitch and Gwen? Well, those two might have been adopted. They're very set in their ways and a bit less tolerant."

"It was sweet of your dad to buy you a home. I'm going to have to keep that story to myself, though. If my mother ever thought such a gift would entice me back to Heartland, she'd most likely figure out a way to buy the entire town."

"It was actually my mother's idea," Noah replied, his tone unintentionally softening at the thought of his mom. She'd been a one of a kind woman. "She died just this side of three years ago. Her final wish was to have all of us home in close proximity."

"There's nothing more important than family," Reese reiterated what was going through Noah's mind. The time she'd taken out of her own life to find closure for another family member spoke volumes. "Well, then. Welcome home, Noah Kendall."

Noah could have been at Tiny's Cavern and enjoying the annual dart championship. He could be getting caught up with old friends. He could have joined his dad at the diner a little bit earlier for a bite to eat. He could have made a call to the state detective to see how much longer it would be before he was able to resume the renovations on his new home. There were a million other things on his plate, but he was at peace sitting next to Reese Woodward for the moment.

"Tell me about yourself," Noah said, giving them another push to obtain that soothing motion she seemed to like so much. "I know a lot about Sophia, but not so much about you."

"According to Chad Schaeffer, everyone knows about me," Reese laughed, although this time she didn't wince. It appeared the pain medicine she'd taken earlier for her headache was finally kicking in. "I'm a high school algebra teacher in Springfield, Illinois. My mother and aunt have always been close, so they made sure they married locally and stayed in town together. They raised us kids together, alternate Sunday dinner, and will most likely be those two old ladies sitting in their rocking chairs gossiping about their neighbors till the end."

"And your dad?" Noah didn't recall Reese talking much about her father. "Is he still in the picture?"

"He is," Reese responded with affection, her warm smile indicating how much she adored him. "My dad works for the telephone company as a technician. He and my mom have been married for thirty-four years. He still brings her home flowers every Friday with his paycheck deposit stub. It's earned him a kiss every Friday afternoon for thirty plus years. The local florist has his selection ready by three o'clock each Friday."

"It sounds like you have wonderful childhood memories." It was no wonder that Reese considered Sophia more like a sister than a cousin. They had been virtually raised in the same house. "After what happened today, anyone would understand your desire to leave Blyth Lake and go home."

"I'm not leaving, Noah. Not like this. Not with that animal still out there." Reese straightened her back and slowly drew her eyes across the darkened landscape. Her determination was visible, but she could likely stoke more fires than the authorities could ever contain. She wasn't his responsibility, but damned if he didn't feel accountable for what her future held while she stayed in town. "I believe there's a connection between Emma and Sophia. I'm going to find out what it is. That man either knows what happened or did the deed himself."

Noah sighed inaudibly, not wanting her to take his reaction the wrong way. He began telling stories of his own childhood memories, painting a picture of his family and the town. He gave her a better understanding of how close knit this community was and their interwoven lives. This wasn't a place where dark deeds were done. It was a town that Norman Rockwell could have painted his pictures in. It was Hometown USA, just like the one she'd grown up in.

Time slowly passed, kept only by the consistent trips the deputy made by the cottage every seven minutes. It was an odd measure of time, but it kept up her smile with each lap.

Reese surprised him by gently resting her head against his shoulder while he kept the swing in motion. He reminded himself that she was only here for a short time, regardless of what additional questions she might uncover in her quest to find the truth. She had a life to get back to in Springfield, while he was just beginning a new one here. They both had anchors, but none of that seemed to matter as she rested her palm on the back of his hand lying on his leg.

"Thank you for staying here with me, Noah."

CHAPTER FOURTEEN

REESE WOKE UP to a myriad of delicious smells—the smoky hickory scent of bacon, French roast coffee, and toasted sourdough bread.

She slowly rolled over with a sly smile and gradually opened just one eye, giving her mind time to clear itself to remember the night's events. Her headache had faded and her cut wasn't near as sensitive. All in all, she wasn't doing too bad this morning. That didn't mean she felt good enough for her daily run. Another day off wouldn't kill all her hard work, but it smelled like the breakfast that was cooking in her kitchen might.

On second thought, that was a bad choice of words. She forgave herself as she inhaled those delightful scents once more.

The sun was shining in through the window and there was a morning dove who was doing his best to let her know that morning was slipping away. He'd gotten into the habit the day after she'd unpacked. At this point, she was debating on whether or not to buy a bird feeder and a hook to hang it on from Calvin Arlo's store. It was possible that type of offering would keep the dove busy until a later hour.

"You going to sleep the day away in there? Aren't teachers supposed to be early risers?"

Reese wasn't the giggling type, but she couldn't suppress them at Noah's question. How in the world had he known she was awake?

"You made breakfast. Is this some kind of country tradition?" Reese made sure her voice carried into the kitchen. Her bedroom was located at the back of the house, making it easy to talk to someone in another room. She tossed her covers back and swung her legs over the side of the bed. She quickly grabbed a change of clothes, making her way to the attached bathroom. "I might have to keep you around if you do this every morning."

Reese had meant to be funny, but the double meaning wasn't lost on her. Damn it. She closed the door and leaned up against the hard wood, waiting for him to reply. There was only silence.

Why had she said something so stupid?

"Hey, keep those butterfly stitches dry," Noah said with a knock. Her clothes fell to the floor as she rested a hand over her heart. Was he trying to give her a heart attack? "I heard Julie say you should wait a couple days before getting them wet."

"I'll be careful," Reece called out, unsure how she managed to keep her tone steady. She leaned down and hastily snatched up her clothes, stepping forward and setting them on the edge of the sink. "Thanks for the reminder. I'll be out in a minute."

Neither one of them referred to her earlier statement. Last night had been nice in many ways, but that didn't mean he was interested in pursuing a relationship of any kind. Having someone to talk to while swinging on the porch swing had been nothing more than a moment in time. The benefit was knowing someone else was there in the event the man who attacked her yesterday tried to finish the job.

Reese really shouldn't make more out of it than that. Noah was an upstanding man with the manners of a gentleman. He may have felt bound to protect her from her unknown assailant.

She listened carefully for the sounds of him walking away, but she didn't hear the boards creak under his rock-solid frame. Holding her breath was only going to last so long.

Reese exhaled quietly and then turned on the water in the sink, which must have drowned out his departure. She took her time brushing her teeth and taking a bath instead of a shower so as to guarantee her cut wouldn't get wet. She even carefully washed her hair without too many acrobatics. She didn't want to seem in a hurry to join him, but then again she didn't want him to think she didn't appreciate him making her breakfast either.

These kinds of situations were always a delicate balance.

Reese walked into the kitchen twenty-five minutes later to find Noah pouring syrup over a stack of pancakes. The delectable sight had her mouth watering in anticipation. She was glad she didn't take time to blow dry her hair. She'd untangled the wet strands and let them hang over her shoulder.

"I could have sworn I didn't have any pancake mix in the cabinets."

Reese took the proffered cup of coffee with a mumbled *thank you*, noting that it was just the right color with the added creamer. He spoke before she could ask how he knew that little bit of information. Was it wrong that it made her feel so special?

"You didn't, but you have all the ingredients to make the batter." Noah surprised her when he stepped forward, leaving not even an inch of space between them as he carefully studied her injury. He gently brushed his thumb underneath the cut as if it received his seal of approval. "It's looking good. You're a fast healer."

Reese nodded, unable to collect her voice.

She should have looked away, but she didn't.

Time stood still.

There was no doubt his intention was to kiss her. His blue eyes drifted down to her lips, which she parted involuntarily in anticipation. Her heart raced, and she had to tighten the grip on the mug in her hand to keep from dropping it. The warm fingers he'd used to caress her forehead now cupped her face.

This was it.

There was no turning back.

And she didn't want to.

"Hello?" A knock sounded on the screen door, prompting both of them to instantly step back. The rush of adrenaline from almost tasting his lips made her lightheaded. "Ms. Woodward? Are you in there?"

"Yes," Reese said loudly, after clearing her throat. She pasted a smile on her face as Calvin Arlo opened the screen door and walked into the house. He didn't even blink at Noah's presence. "Good morning. Did you make it through the night alright?"

She wasn't sure why Calvin would have reason to stop by. He'd never done so before, and his visit now had her questioning his motives. She didn't believe that he was the one who attacked her in the restroom yesterday, but that didn't mean he wasn't the one behind it.

Was Calvin responsible for what happened to Emma Irwin? Was it somehow connected to Sophia and her disappearance?

"Rose caught me before I went fishing this morning." Calvin adjusted his ball cap as he nodded his head in greeting toward Noah. "She wanted me to bring over an air conditioning unit for your bedroom window. I cut enough lumber to secure the bracket so no one can take the unit out from the outside. That way, you can secure the house at night and not worry about unwanted visitors. I also got this old pump 16-gauge scatter gun if you want it. It'd be enough to deter most folks. I got it topped off with a hot load of buckshot shells."

Reese relaxed somewhat at his explanation, accepting that she'd let her mind run away from her there for a minute. She hadn't realized she'd stepped closer to Noah until she sensed his left hand resting on her lower back.

"I'm glad to see you're watching over her, Noah." Calvin glanced at his watch that had seen better days. "I'll get this installed and then out of y'all's hair. You shouldn't have to worry about any press coming back through here for a day or two. Pete Anderson arrived in town first thing this morning."

"That ought to be a shitstorm." Noah gestured that Reese should sit down and eat her breakfast while it was warm before joining Calvin. "Let me help you with the air unit. We can have you back on your boat within the hour."

"And miss the show going on in town right now? Not on your life. If Pete Anderson is responsible for killing that sweet girl and stuffing her body into his wall, I want to be there when they take him away in cuffs."

Reese had lost her appetite. She didn't want Noah to think she didn't appreciate his home cooked breakfast, though. She took a sip of her coffee—which was made to perfection with just the right amount of sugar and cream—and picked up her fork to force a few bites down.

It wasn't that hard to hear Noah and Calvin's conversation about what could have happened twelve years ago, especially considering the older man's deep voice traveled easily.

Why would Pete Anderson come back to town if he were the guilty party? That made no sense, and honestly, Reese didn't have it in her this morning to sort it out. The detectives would take care of that, and hopefully also find a link to Sophia.

It hit her then that maybe she should reach out to the lead detective. She couldn't recall his name, but Noah had his number. She would bring it up to him later today.

"That should do it," Calvin announced, walking back into the kitchen around thirty minutes later. She'd eaten what she could and had just finished rinsing off her plate. "It's a simple unit, so you shouldn't have any trouble using it. Just make sure the door is shut to keep the cool air inside your bedroom or the unit will freeze up and the compressor will overheat."

"I appreciate it." Reese smiled and crossed the kitchen to shake his hand. "I'll call Rose and thank her as well."

"We look after our own." Calvin clapped Noah on the back before taking his leave. "I'm heading to the diner for some breakfast. You two enjoy your day. I left the shotgun in the corner behind the door in your bedroom."

The house fell quiet as Calvin left the two of them alone.

The heat of Noah's gaze on her was hotter than had she been standing outside in the blazing sun. It was as if the half hour apart hadn't done a thing to dampen her attraction to him, but it did give her time to second guess herself.

She'd been so prepared to live a little wildly, but now it just seemed reckless.

She was only here for another month.

"I was thinking that maybe I should talk to that detective who was at your house the other day." Reese turned back toward the sink and lifted the handle on the faucet, more to give herself something to do. She didn't want to say something foolish she couldn't take back. She really enjoyed his company and would like their friendship to continue, but getting involved would be a mistake. She was conflicted. It was nice to have someone to talk to about why she was here, but she would have to go home eventually. "I could explain why I think there's a connection between Sophia and Emma's disappearances."

Noah didn't reply right away. She waited while she looked out the window toward the edge of the tree line, not expecting the heat from his body to envelop her from behind. Her breath caught when he rested the palms of his hands on either side of her against the counter.

Was he trying to induce a heart attack with his body?

She couldn't recall a time she'd ever been so physically attracted to a man, but even that thought fled as his warm breath caressed her ear. The rich tone of his voice evoked an arousal that could have set her clothes on fire.

"We have two choices here." Reese found herself mesmerized as he reached out and slowly pushed the faucet down until the water stopped running over the dishes. He shouldn't have done that. Her heartrate had tripled. "Look at me, sweetheart."

He called her sweetheart.

There went any good intentions she might have had for the last few days.

Reese slowly turned, though Noah remained just as close as he had before. With his hands resting on the counter, he'd made sure he was at eye level. She'd always loved the color blue.

"I want you." Noah's penetrating gaze remained steady on hers, not leaving any doubt as to which way he wanted this conversation to end. "I know you have a life in Springfield to get back to, and that you're here just for the summer. But that doesn't mean we can't enjoy what time we have together."

Reese couldn't find her voice. The men she'd dated in the past didn't possess an ounce of Noah's magnetism. She was, quite honestly, afraid she'd lose herself in this so-called vacation and never want to return to her life in Springfield.

"Or we can maintain this budding friendship and ignore what we both truly want."

He was waiting for her to decide. The lightheadedness she'd experienced earlier came back with a vengeance. The decision was in her hands, and they were coated with perspiration.

She answered by leaning forward a half-inch, lightly pressing her lips to his.

She was a goner.

Lightning didn't literally strike her dead, but it was damn

close.

His response to her offer was immediate. He lifted his hands and slipped his fingers into her still-damp strands, holding her still so that he could taste her properly.

He did more than that.

There was kissing, and then there was…*being taken.*

It was all-consuming.

He was all-consuming.

He continued to kiss her as if the sun would never set. The strokes of his tongue were sensual, his lips caressed hers, and all she could do was respond in kind.

Noah leaned into her so that there was no space between their bodies, giving her the ability to wrap her arms around his neck. There was no pulling him closer, but that didn't mean she didn't try.

She couldn't get enough of the slight mint taste of his tongue that had become most addictive. Never in a million years had she thought coffee could be replaced, but she'd just been proven wrong.

Her body vibrated in places that had previously ached, reminding her that they could do so much more lying down in the cool air circulating around in her bedroom. She slipped her right hand into his dark hair, signaling that she was ready to move this into the other room. The pulsations she'd sensed only became stronger.

Reese tore her lips from his, using the momentary break to catch her breath.

"Is that your phone?"

"Yes," Noah answered regrettably, pulling his cell from the front pocket of his jeans. "It's Detective Kendrick."

Noah swiped his screen and took the call, though he didn't step away from her. It was obvious he was listening intently to what the detective had to say, but that didn't stop him from playing with her drying hair. He wrapped one lock around his finger over and over again while the simple, unconscious act caused her to want him even more.

"Really? That's great news."

Reese closed her eyes in response to Noah's lips against the sensitive part of her neck. She rested her forehead against his chest, trying to listen to what he was saying while experiencing jolts of arousal travel through her body at the simplest of gestures.

"Yes, I can do that."

Noah paused long enough to catch her earlobe between his teeth, nipping ever so lightly.

"I appreciate the call, but I do have someone here who would like to discuss something with you."

The turn of the tables Noah just executed had Reese biting her tongue to prevent her from saying something scathing. Yes, she wanted to talk to the detective about Sophia. Yes, it was the reason she was in Blyth Lake.

But that didn't mean it had to be done now, when every nerve in her body had been awakened after a long slumber.

Noah didn't have much luck hiding his grin as she grabbed the phone from his hand and stepped to the side. Unlike him, she couldn't be in such a compromising position while talking with an officer of the law.

"Detective Kendrick? This is Reese Woodward. I was hoping to discuss something that I believe might be connected to Emma Irwin's disappearance."

Reese listened as the detective cautioned that they didn't have conclusive evidence that the remains belonged to Emma, but he was willing to meet with her to discuss her concerns. The timing worked out well, considering he wanted to speak with

Pete Anderson while the man was in town.

"I'll meet you for lunch at Annie's Diner around noon, if that's alright."

"Yes, that would perfect." Reese wasn't the only one who heard the rumble of an engine. It sounded familiar, but Noah was the one to see who had come calling this early in the morning. It wasn't lost on her that he let his hand stroke her back on his way by to the screen door. "I'll see you then."

"Looks like you have another visitor, Reese," Noah said, interest lacing his tone with something else she couldn't put her finger on. "You're a popular woman this morning."

Reese closed the distance between them, standing shoulder to shoulder with Noah. Who had caught his interest, and why had he become so tense?

"Oh," Reese said in surprise. "Wait. Isn't he one of the medics who treated me yesterday?"

"Yes. And I highly doubt he's here to see how you're doing,"

Noah opened the screen door and stepped outside. He waited for her to join him. For some reason, she got the idea that he didn't want Billy Stanton inside the house.

"Noah, is there something you need to tell me about Billy?"

CHAPTER FIFTEEN

NOAH WAITED FOR Billy to get out of his brand new red Mustang Shelby GT350. It wasn't surprising to see that the richest kid in town grew up to be a wealthy adult, though the medic sideline had been a bit of a surprise.

Just three years ago, Billy had been going to medical school to follow in his father's footsteps. Looked like that hadn't turned out too well for the man. As for Dr. Stanton, he maintained a luxury apartment in Cleveland and flew his own Cessna Citation CJ4 home every other weekend. It worked for them, but it certainly wasn't a lifestyle Noah would choose under any circumstances.

Who spent six and a half million on their own personal jet aircraft, and then only flew it a couple times a month? The Stanton family estate had its own landing strip north of town, although it was still within the county line.

Their continuous six hundred and forty acres comprised an entire section of prime Ohio farmland that hadn't been tilled in fifty plus years—not one single acre. Most of the estate had been replanted with native hardwood trees during the '50s. What few barns remained on the property were strictly used for riding horses and storing equipment.

The hangar alone was large enough to store not only Dr. Stanton's Citation, but a completely restored P51-D Mustang World War II fighter aircraft.

As far as anyone knew, the good doctor hadn't flown the Mustang but once, the tale went that the flight scared him so bad that he never managed to work up enough courage to give the P51-D another try.

The main house was massive in size, just over eighteen thousand square feet. The property line was enclosed by what seemed like an endless five-foot-tall split rail fence painted a distinctive Navajo red. One couldn't drive past the place without seeing that damned fence running on for a mile on all four sides.

He and Billy had never been what one might consider friends, partly due to the fact that Billy was a year younger and had been a class behind him. Most people tolerated him because his family brought a shitload of money into the county. Noah took issue with how Billy flaunted his family's wealth. That was frowned upon in these parts where most folks had to work hard to earn a decent living.

"Noah, your old man told me I'd find you here," Billy said in greeting with a flashy smile almost as bright as the wide white stripe painted down the middle of his shiny red sports car. There wasn't a strand of his blond hair out of place. "I was hoping we could talk about the property."

Noah had to have heard Stanton wrong, but he hadn't stuttered. Billy now set his sights on Reese, which really wasn't a surprise considering the man had expressed his interest in her yesterday. She'd been too worried about her attacker to think that one of the medics treating her would resort to that kind of salacious behavior while in uniform.

"Ms. Woodward," Billy said, making his way to the bottom of the porch steps. He twirled his keyring on his index finger and caught them in the palm of his hand. "I'm glad to see you're feeling better."

"Thank you." Reese was a very intelligent woman, and she

hadn't missed the underlying tension.

"Are you talking about my property up the road there?" Noah ignored Billy's hidden meaning in his words. He'd been a nuisance in high school, but he was crossing a line he didn't even know was right in front of him. "What interest is it of yours?"

Reese still maintained a hold on Noah's cell phone as she made her way to the porch swing. She sat down, close enough to hear the conversation.

"Well, you see, your father bought the property at auction." Billy rested one of his loafers on the second step. His arrogant air dimmed a bit as he got down to business. "Honestly, I'm hoping you'll sell. I'll give you an additional twenty percent above market price, even with all that has happened recently."

"Why would I do that?"

"Come on," Billy said with a laugh, switching his gaze between Noah and Reese in bewilderment. "You can't be serious? You can't tell me that you wouldn't have a problem living in a house where a body has been stored for…what? Twelve years?"

"Those remains are most likely from someone we all knew, Billy." Noah wasn't in the mood to play word games with someone he didn't particularly care for, so he brought the conversation to a close. "The property is not for sale, no matter what offer you bring to the table. It will remain in my family for many years to come."

Billy pulled his lips down in disappointment, but he rose his hands in surrender.

"Fine, Kendall." Billy lifted the sunglasses he had dangling from his shirt and slipped them up the bridge of his nose. "Should you change your mind, you know where to find me. Ms. Woodward."

And with a leisurely nod in Reese's direction to bid her goodbye, Billy casually made his way to his car. It wasn't long before he fired up his 5.2 liter v8 engine. He backed his Mustang out of the driveway and headed toward town.

"You didn't once let on yesterday that you hated the guy," Reese said, still pushing the swing with her bare foot.

Her pink toenail polish reminded him that the day could have been spent having a lot more fun in her bed enjoying the new air conditioning unit than driving into town to meet with Detective Kendrick where everyone and their mother would be congregating at the diner. They'd all be ordering lunch at the exact same time, never letting on that they were trying to hear what was new in the case.

"Hate is an awful strong word." Noah joined her on the porch swing, resting his arm behind her as they both allowed this morning's events to settle back into an easy rhythm. "I can usually tolerate Billy under most normal conditions. Let's just say I'm a little on edge today, given the circumstances."

Reese fell silent and rather still, her hands resting in her lap. It was then he realized that she'd taken his sentiment the wrong way.

"Hey," Noah said softly, reaching over and using his fingers to lift her chin. He didn't like the doubt that filled her brown eyes. "I'm all in regarding where we left off in the kitchen. I was referring to what happened yesterday and the fact that you want to speak with Kendrick about what got you attacked in the first place."

"You think I'm making myself an even bigger target when in fact I'm releasing the pressure which caused the incident." Reese lifted an arm and squeezed his hand in reassurance. "If Kendrick starts investigating a connection between Sophia and Emma, then there's no reason to come after me again. The information is already out there, and hurting me would gain whoever attacked me yesterday nothing but more grief."

Noah highly doubted a man who would assault a woman in public thought in those kinds of terms, but he'd be around to ensure her safety.

"So let me get this straight. You scheduled us to meet Detective Kendrick in town where everyone will be eavesdropping when we could have spent the day seeing how well your new air conditioning unit works?"

Reese twisted her lips sideways as if she were thinking through the roadblock she'd set up when they heard another vehicle approaching.

"You've got to be kidding me," Noah muttered, catching sight of a media van driving down the lane and bypassing Reese's house. "You get more traffic through here than Grand Central Station. I thought Calvin said that the press would be too preoccupied with Pete Anderson to come out this way."

"I'm sure the backdrop of the farmhouse adds to the visual of the segment. They'll probably just green screen the farm into the background. At least one of the deputies is down that way to prevent the reporters from getting too close to your house." They continued to monitor the media van until it faded from view. "That reminds me, you never did say why the detective called you to begin with."

"I was a little distracted by someone." As much as Noah wanted to use what hours they had to take what they'd started into the bedroom, he didn't like that the media was now canvassing his property. "Kendrick said that forensics has given the all clear. I can restart the renovation work at the farm tomorrow."

Noah wasn't sure how Reese would take that news, especially considering she'd been quite uncomfortable with the fact that he still planned to restore and move into the farmhouse after finding the probable remains of Emma Irwin.

"You know we're technically on two strikes," Reese pointed out with a sigh. Noah gave her a questioning look. "Both occasions I've spent time with you ended up with the police being called to our location. You sure you want to go for a third time at bat?"

Noah pushed the swing with his work boot a little harder than she was anticipating, but that was his intention as she caught herself before she fell out of the swing. He sat on the cushion when it rebounded and pulled her in his lap, waiting patiently until she stopped laughing from being out of breath.

"Call me a risk taker, little one," Noah ordered as he wiggled his eyebrows, emitting a growl as he feigned biting her neck. Reese's sweet laughter rang out a little louder until it transformed into a pleasurable moan. "Kiss me, sweetheart."

Noah wasn't expecting Reese to shift position. She straddled him in that free spirit he'd caught glimpses of every now and then. She cradled his face in the palms of her hands as she took the lead, doing her best to convince him that they should ignore everything going on next door and in town in favor of going to her bedroom and locking the world out.

Reese pulled away to rest her forehead against his as his cell phone rang from where it had dropped between them. There were simply times when one needed to wave the white flag. The current was pushing against them.

"I'll go brush my hair and change clothes." Reese reluctantly put one bare foot on the porch and then the other. The world had come knocking on their door, leaving them no choice but to answer. "Let's just hope we can get through the day without an emergency call being placed to the sheriff."

Noah couldn't help but observe the sway of Reese's hips as she made her way to the screen door. He hoped like hell they could pull off what she'd most likely jinxed with her humor.

He'd noticed earlier that the deputy hadn't been by since they'd been outside this morning.

Something told him that today wasn't going to go as smooth as they'd like it to in their bid for a little peace and quiet.

REESE SHOULD HAVE excused herself long ago and taken the shortcut back to her house. Nothing out of the ordinary had happened today, proving that her attacker had most likely moved on to bigger and better things. Her meeting with Detective Kendrick had been overtly public, allowing anyone at the diner to overhear what she had to say.

She could no longer even pretend to conceal her reason for being in Blyth Lake, not that anyone had caused her to do so to begin with. She'd done so out of courtesy and respect to those who had put Emma's disappearance behind them.

What she *had* thought would be kept more personal was the intimacy that had developed between her and Noah.

Having dinner with his father, Gus Kendall, didn't exactly fulfill that objective.

All eyes were on them as they sat at a table in the middle of the diner.

"He doesn't bite much," Noah murmured in her ear as he feigned reaching for the shaker of salt.

Reese shot Noah a sideways look of irritation, wishing he'd finish his meal so that they could get out of Dodge. It didn't help that Whitney Bell was currently in the booth beside them with a man who looked like he'd just escaped a prison yard riot.

"I was thinking of grilling up some barbeque chicken tomorrow." Gus took a sip of the water he'd asked for to accompany his club sandwich. "Why don't the two of you head over to the house around five o'clock?"

What had Noah said to prompt Gus to include her in his invitation? She'd been very careful of how she acted around Noah all afternoon. One should think they were just neighbors and friends, but somehow their relationship had been consigned to something more intimate.

"I actually have—"

"We'll be there," Noah said, cutting off the excuse she'd drummed up in her head that was more than plausible to extricate herself from a family obligation. How was this normal that he wasn't fazed in the least by the interest they were generating? "I'd also like to talk to you about designs for the new cupboards now that I got that wall out of the way."

The chimes above the door sounded and in walked an older woman who immediately drew applause and cheers. She used a cane, but there was a liveliness about her that couldn't be contained. She patted her grey hair as if she were the belle of the ball.

"Mama, what are you doing here?" Cassie exclaimed as she made her way out of the kitchen to see what all the fuss was about. "Didn't Darcy take you to your doctor's appointment in the city?"

The older woman narrowed her eyes at the fact that her daughter just announced to the town her personal business. Reese commiserated with the woman over that lost battle.

"I still have my faculties, Cassie. Yes, Darcy took me to see Dr. Stanton. Then I decided he could drop me off here for a bite of dinner." Reese didn't have to have it spelled out for her. This woman was the infamous Annie Osburn. "He'll be joining me shortly, as a matter of fact."

Multiple townsfolk started talking at once, many asking about Annie's health and what she'd been doing with her downtime. Gus used a napkin to wipe his mouth before excusing himself to help Annie with her chair at a nearby table.

"My mom used to say Dad had a crush on Ms. Osburn," Noah said with fondness, looking on as his father set the handle of the cane on the table so that it was within reach. "It was a running joke in the family, especially when Mom would make meatloaf. We called them meatloaf wars."

She would have responded had Annie Osburn not made eye contact. The woman's penetrating stare caused Reese to shift uncomfortably in her chair.

"Relax." If Noah was trying to get out from under Reese's ire, he wasn't doing a good job of it. "You, of all people, should know how small towns work. Rumors were probably rife yesterday after word got around that we were at the beach together. Throw in Calvin catching me at your house this morning all but solidified that we're having a secret love child by this point."

Reese was well aware Noah was right in every aspect, but that didn't mean she wanted to become grist for the gossip mill.

"I'm just saying that we don't have to help those rumors along." She kept her voice low, not wanting Whitney to hear any more than she already had. Reese glanced back at Noah to find him studying her. "What?"

"I do like the way you're wearing your hair." Noah rested his piercing blue eyes on her, effectively raising the temperature in the diner. They both pushed their plates away. "It looks like Dad found another dinner companion. What do you say we bid him goodnight and head out?"

Reese thought this moment would never come, and she wouldn't hesitate in taking him up on his offer now. She hadn't consciously left her hair down in the long, natural waves she'd gotten from her mother, though she had worn a pair of white capris and a yellow blouse that was nicer than most of the stuff she'd packed in her suitcase. She'd wanted to make a better impression in front of the detective than she had originally.

Appearances went a long way toward a person's character when one wanted to be believed.

Noah pulled out his wallet and left enough cash on the table to cover all three meals. Reese didn't doubt that he would argue with her should she offer her share, so she pushed back her chair and grabbed her purse. She'd gotten into the habit of only carrying her cell phone and credit card, but today's meeting with Detective Kendrick had called for pictures of Sophia. Those were easier to carry in her purse.

"Ms. Woodward. I was hoping to have a word with you." Reese fought off the shiver of unease that accompanied Annie Osburn's invitation. The elderly lady was smiling, but there was something off about her request. "If you would, please?"

Reese wasn't the only one who found Ms. Osburn's summons odd. Noah frowned in his father's direction, almost as if he were blaming his dad for this delay.

She didn't believe Gus Kendall had anything to do with Annie Osburn wanting to speak with her, and Reese immediately recalled a horror movie where an elderly woman went around killing young women who were interested in her son. It was odd what one thought of in situations like these.

This was nothing like that, but that didn't mean Reese was that off base with Ms. Osburn's sudden attention.

"I'm sorry," Reese said in an attempt to find out what she was getting herself into before sitting in front of a match after she'd pretty much been doused with gasoline. "I don't believe we've met."

"We haven't yet," Annie agreed, settling back in her chair as Cassie set a hot cup of tea on the table. The younger woman mouthed her apology before heading back toward the kitchen. "But I did, in fact, meet your cousin, Sophia. Twelve years ago, to be precise."

CHAPTER SIXTEEN

NOAH PULLED BACK on the lever to dim the bright headlights of his truck as he drove down the dirt road. Hitting the brights in a case like this only made the dirt floating in the air seem thicker. Reese had been quiet ever since her conversation with Annie Osburn had come to a conclusion. He didn't blame her.

"I can give Lance a call to confirm what Ms. Osburn said for you tonight," Noah offered, wishing he had the power to take away Reese's confusion. "She might have her facts wrong. She is getting on in years."

"Ms. Osburn isn't wrong." Reese finally stopped looking out the passenger side window and focused on him. Her movement allowed him to see that she was still as strong-willed as ever. The dashboard lights illuminated her determination to find answers. "*She* is the reason Sophia went to camp that year. What I don't understand is why Tanner didn't tell me the whole truth."

"Tanner is Sophia's brother, right?" Noah turned into her small driveway, ignoring the temptation to check on his place. Deputy Wallace was back on duty, so he should have things covered for the night. "It couldn't hurt to call him to verify what you've been told. Besides, Ms. Osburn might have misread the situation completely."

Annie Osburn had been born Anastasia Pearl Osburn. The older generation easily recalled the time Annie packed her bags at the young age of nineteen and headed off to Hollywood. She starred in a very popular movie as a secondary character, and even starred in a few commercials. It wasn't until she was in her mid to late twenties that she came back to town with Cassie in tow, never speaking of her time away from Blyth Lake to anyone who Noah knew of firsthand.

"Annie didn't misread anything," Reese said with a woeful smile. "Sophia sought her out so that she could find her way into the movie business. Everyone back home always thought it was a pipe dream, even with her exceptional looks."

"You said yourself that Sophia wouldn't have left home without saying goodbye. Her relationship with her father might have been strained, but your cousin loved you very much from what you've told me about her." Noah had turned the key and cut the engine. There were a few clicks and pops from the exhaust manifold cooling. This wasn't how he'd intended to end this evening. "Call Tanner."

Reese made no attempt to exit the truck. She reached down for her purse that was next to her yellow flowered sandals. Her cell phone was in her hand when she sat back, but she didn't call her cousin.

"I think..." Reese's voice trailed off as she struggled to find the right words.

Noah didn't want Reese to spend her night unable to sleep because she didn't make a simple phone call.

"Call him, Reese," Noah urged, reaching over to her and pushing back the light brown strands he'd been admiring all day and night.

"What I want is you. I just want to forget for a little while. Is that so bad?"

Speaking of desire, that lone emotion was deep and raw in her tone.

He would give her anything in this moment.

Reese surprised him when she set her phone up on the dashboard and pressed the button on her seatbelt. She kicked off those bright sandals before she climbed over the console. She was petite enough to fit perfectly between him and the steering wheel.

The clouds parted, allowing the soft moonlight to enter the cab of his truck and shine down on her like a spotlight.

Damn, but she was beautiful.

It was she who could be the next star in a Hollywood movie.

"Not here," Noah said with a shake of his head. She'd already lifted his t-shirt away from his jeans. She sure as hell wasn't making this easy. He leaned his head back when she stroked her fingers across his abdomen. "If you recall, you have a brand-new air conditioning unit we need to operationally test extensively."

"Where's that risk taker you were telling me about?" Reese whispered, leaning forward and capturing his lips. It should have been the other way around. This was not how he pictured their first time together, and now she was throwing his own words back in his face. "Take a risk with me, Mr. Kendall."

Reese sounded so overconfident in her ability to get him to act on impulse that he couldn't resist her challenge.

Noah had his shirt and the holster attached to his waistband off within seconds, keeping the latter within reach. The gentle beams from the moon highlighted her excited gaze, making it seem as if the golden flecks in her eyes glowed in anticipation.

They might be making love in the cab of his truck, but that didn't mean it had to be quick. He stopped her attempt at unfastening the button of his jeans. He didn't miss the catch in her breath when he slowly raised her arms so that it was easy for him to remove her shirt.

"You're not wearing a bra, little one."

"No, I'm not," Reese agreed in a seductive tone that took him by surprise.

Noah would never have pictured her the teasing type, but he really, really liked this side of her.

"Have you thought about what will happen when Deputy Wallace drives this way to check on you?"

Noah couldn't contain his laugh when her arms suddenly came down and crisscrossed over her body. This was a hell of a lot more fun than he would have thought.

"We'll duck," Noah murmured, tangling his fingers in her hair and drawing her closer. He melded his lips to hers and kissed her thoroughly before exploring what was right in front of him. "You are so beautiful."

Reese leaned back against the steering wheel, arching her back to give him better access to her breasts. He palmed her ample flesh, brushing each thumb over her nipples. They hardened in response, but it was her enticing moan that had an arousing effect on him.

He took her right nipple in his mouth, suckling the nub gently as he continued to caress her other. She shifted and her hair became a shield as he continued to make love to her body.

Noah unfastened the button on her capris with his left hand, but purposefully left her wanting. He wasn't even remotely done pleasuring her. Their current positions made it rather hard to do the things he wanted, so he improvised.

The driver's seat was already as far back as it could go, but he reached around her and pulled the lever that had the steering wheel tilting upward. He wrapped his hands around her waist and easily shifted her so that she was facing forward.

"Now I have better access," Noah whispered, catching her earlobe in between his teeth. He stroked his hands down the front of her until he was able to shimmy the fabric of both her capris and panties down until the material slipped over her knees. He was relatively sure she was able to get one ankle free. "Put your foot up on the dashboard, sweetheart."

Reese leaned back against him and turned her head to capture his lips. She had done as he'd requested, opening herself up to him as she lifted her arms and wrapped her hands around the headrest.

Noah noted her change in breathing when he lightly brushed his fingers down the front of her and into her folds. He kissed her shoulders as he stroked her sensitive clitoris, loving how she pressed into him to lift her hips in anticipation.

"You are so wet."

"I want you," Reese said, lowering her right arm and resting her hand over his in an attempt to rush things along. He wasn't having any of it. "Please, Noah."

"We have all night."

Noah used his finger to breach her entrance, cherishing the gasp that fell from her lips. He withdrew, only to then re-enter her to elicit another alluring reaction. He'd hardened to the point of pain, but the end result would be worth the wait.

Her dainty toes painted in that pretty pink nail polish curled when he added another finger, rubbing against her sweet spot. The change in her breathing was audible, raising his own need to draw out her orgasm.

"Noah, I—"

"Come for me," Noah requested softly, loving the way her sheath tightened on his fingers upon his wanting appeal. "That's right, sweetheart. Take what you need."

Reese's hips lifted in response, her release coming in waves as well as the tantalizing whimpers that made him want more. Her grip on the headrest had tilted the seat slightly forward. He showered her shoulder with gentle kisses until she'd regained her composure.

Her next statement was music to his ears.

"I want more."

CHAPTER SEVENTEEN

R EESE NEVER IN a million years would have thought she'd be making love in the cab of a pickup truck at her age. She wasn't sure what had come over her when Noah had pulled the truck into her driveway. He had a way of making her laugh, causing her frustrations to evaporate, and then a second later make her want him in a way she'd never wanted another man.

It wasn't that she didn't want the romance or the comfort of her bed.

They sure as hell would have been cooler had they taken this into the bedroom with the new AC unit and all.

But she couldn't wait.

She was like a woman in the desert, and she had to have that tall drink of cool water.

She had to have him, and he didn't disappoint in any way.

Noah took his time exploring her body and was an expert on how to bring pleasure to a woman with his hands.

Now she wanted *him*.

Reese lowered her left leg from the dashboard, not so sure she had the strength to shift her body weight. She fought through the overwhelming desire to stay where she was in his embrace. It wasn't until she was once again straddling him that she found the rest of her voice.

"Please tell me you have a condom on you."

Noah's smile was her answer as he slightly lifted himself in order to reach his wallet. The movement caused the rough metal zipper of his jeans to brush against her clitoris. She bit her lip and closed her eyes to keep from crying out in a mix of pleasure and pain.

"I might not have been a Boy Scout, but I always come prepared," Noah teased, holding up the foiled package in victory. One kiss as a reward was all it took to send the stimulation meter through the roof. "You're like a sip of fresh lemonade on a sweltering day, Reese Woodward. I just can't get enough."

The cab of the truck *was* hot, causing their skin to stick together and the humidity to rise. The windows had fogged over long ago, but she didn't care. Her body wasn't recognizing anything other than his sensual touch.

"Here," Reese murmured, taking the condom and lifting herself up on her knees so that he could push his jeans and briefs down his thighs. He could only manage to get them down so far, but it was more than enough. "I think it's about to get hotter in here."

That was an understatement. His shaft was thick and long, causing her to want to delay the inevitable. She would have loved to have done a little exploration of her own, but he took the decision out of her hands.

"Another time," Noah promised, ripping the foil with his teeth before extracting the latex. He covered himself fully and then tossed the empty package to the side. His large hands wrapped around her waist, lifting her up so that his tip was at her entrance. "Take the lead, sweetheart."

He didn't have to encourage her in the least. Reese rested her hands on his wide shoulders, using him as leverage as she slowly lowered herself over him. She once again bit her lip as the intense pleasure of taking him inside of her was overwhelming. It took her a long time to adjust to the sweet burning sensation created by their union.

"You take my breath away." Reese would have expressed a similar sentiment, but Noah kissed her thoroughly until he was fully seated inside of her. They both paused to enjoy this moment, their body heat raising the temperature even more. "I'm telling the medics you're responsible for our deaths."

Reese had never laughed during this type of encounter before, but something about this moment was magical. She lifted herself up before slowly taking him back inside of her, doing so over and over again until the physical ache of need became almost unbearable.

She stared into his blue eyes as they both reached their threshold. The enthralling explosion had them both crying out each other's names, their cries echoing throughout the cab of his truck. Perspiration made it almost impossible for her to hold onto him, so she slapped one hand against the window and grabbed the back of his seat with the other as pleasure rippled throughout her body.

Reese couldn't contain the bubble of laughter.

"Really?" Noah arched an eyebrow, though it was difficult to see his expression in the dark. The fog that covered the windows had created a barrier between the interior and the light from the moon. "I'm not sure that's a compliment."

"I'm sorry," Reese said rather breathlessly, still remaining on top of him as she tried to contain her laughter. She wasn't ready to move and lose their intimate connection. "I was picturing us doing this in the city. It never would have happened."

She finally removed her hand from the window, a sliver of light highlighting his smile in response to the image she'd just created.

"Can we just sleep out here? Better yet, how about in the bed of your truck underneath the stars?" Reese finally shifted to the passenger seat to cool them both down. She brushed her hair out of her face when he didn't respond in kind. An awkward silence filled the cab. "Noah?"

Had she done something wrong?

Reese lifted her shirt to her chest in defense as she tried to figure out what had changed in the last minute.

"Wallace should have driven past your house at least a dozen times by now."

Noah grimaced when he couldn't pull up his jeans without cleaning himself off. He moved his firearm he'd set on the middle console and rummaged around the inside until he came away with a few napkins.

"We *were* a little busy," Reese reminded him after hesitating just a bit. That didn't stop her from hastily throwing on her clothes as fast as she could in preparation of what he was about to suggest. It was the right thing to do, even though this wasn't exactly how she pictured the rest of the night going. "Can't we call the sheriff's office? Maybe Deputy Wallace was called away The sheriff could have told him to stay in front of your farm."

Noah surprised her after he'd finished cleaning up, wadding up the napkins, and getting dressed himself. He pulled her close for a kiss, taking his time to let her know that he'd enjoyed the past hour as much as she had.

"I'll make this up to you." Noah put the discarded trash into a bag in the side pocket of his door, starting the engine at the same time. "We'll call Patty at the station while we driving down that way."

Reese ran her hands through her hair, doing her best to look presentable. Chances were they'd find that Deputy Wallace had fallen asleep on his shift. She didn't want him to draw conclusions based on her rumpled clothes and swollen lips. It dawned on her that yet again they were ending their evening with a police visit.

"You know, we're going to get a reputation if we keep ending each outing with the inclusion of local law enforcement."

Reese shot Noah a smile as he shifted his truck into reverse. They had to wait a few seconds until the windows cleared. Who would have thought that this emotional quest she'd taken upon herself would result in a summer liaison? She'd neglected herself for so long that this much fun was well overdue.

"The Kendalls already have a reputation around these parts," Noah said with a laugh, though his concern for Deputy Wallace was evident. He pressed his cell phone a little closer to his ear. "Yeah, Patty? This is Noah Kendall. I was wondering if Deputy Wallace was called away from his post. I haven't seen him drive by Ms. Woodward's rental since we've returned from dinner."

The short drive down the rock road toward Noah's new place was rather eerie. The clouds kept shifting in front of the moon, thus casting darker shadows on the path in front of them. The leaves were no longer moving on the branches above them, signaling that the light breeze from earlier had dissipated.

"And the sheriff hasn't checked on him?"

Noah's question caught Reese's attention, and suddenly, the wonderful night ahead of them took a turn for the worse.

Something was wrong.

"No, I'm heading that way now," Noah responded to whatever the dispatcher had inquired. "I'll let you know what I find, but you might want to send someone else out this way. You can tell the sheriff that this will be addressed at the next town hall meeting."

"What happened?" Reese asked after Noah disconnected the line and set his phone in the cup holder. "What will you address at the meeting?"

"The fact that the sheriff didn't think it was a problem that

Wallace hasn't called in since his last check-in several hours ago." His anger and frustration was more than evident. The headlights of the truck led the way to the end of the circle, where the deputy's police car was parked with the door wide open. "I want you to stay in this truck with the doors locked. Take my phone and redial the last number I called. Tell Patty to get the sheriff's ass out here now, along with the state police."

The euphoria Reese had recently experienced vanished the second she noticed what caused him to request the police. After all, the car door being left open could have signified that Deputy Wallace had entered the woods in search of someone. It also could have simply been the officer's need to relieve himself. She honestly would have rather caught the deputy with his pants down than to see his body lying prone just outside the beam of the headlights.

This wasn't how she'd pictured their night ending.

Not with them finding another body at Noah's farm.

CHAPTER EIGHTEEN

"I T'S BEEN A little over a week," Gus pointed out from his location in the kitchen. He had been measuring the dimensions of the far wall for the upper cabinets, as well as the walk-in pantry door he was designing to match. It had to open into the room, but he had enough clearance to design a storage system on the reverse side for a broom, a dustpan with a brush, and a three-step lightweight stepstool. He shifted his worn leather tool belt hanging loosely around his waist as he took a small break and drank some of the sweet iced tea Reese had brought them earlier. "No word from that detective on the DNA results at all? On television, they get the results in a half an hour. What's with the state's lab guys?"

A lot had happened in the eight days since Noah and Reese had discovered Deputy Wallace's body at the turnaround near the DNR wetlands at the edge of Noah's property. The man's funeral had been a couple of days ago, delayed due to the required autopsy by the state investigators. He'd been shot in the chest with a 9mm firearm.

The governor had sent a special assistant prosecutor from his office to facilitate anything the state's forensics team needed, considering a county sheriff's deputy had been murdered. They were moving heaven and earth to see justice done. After all that, the only thing they could say for certain was that Deputy Wallace was dead before he ever hit the ground.

"I spoke to Detective Kendrick yesterday." Noah decided he could use a break, as well. He leaned down and used the wall as leverage, taking a seat on the floor. The two additional walls, the carpet, and pretty much the entire kitchen had been gutted. There was nothing left but studs and the wiring for the existing sockets which he would have to change to GFCI due to code changes after they were originally installed. It gave him something to do while waiting for some much-needed answers. "The DNA results aren't back from the lab. As for Deputy Wallace's murder, there are no leads at this time. The sheriff had yet to install the dashboard cams that were provided by the state for all marked squad cars last quarter. They sure as hell would have come in handy in this case. I'm telling you, Dad, Sheriff Percy's job performance leaves a lot to be desired. He's just plain neglectful."

"You aren't telling me anything I don't already know." Gus set his glass on the counter, the leftover ice cubes clinking against the sides. "The entire town is up in arms and calling for his immediate resignation."

Reese's laughter drifted through the open door. Rose and Tiny had stopped by with an invitation to the Cavern. They were having a celebration and handing the keys for the place over to Brynn Mercer. The symbolic event had been scheduled a while ago, but they'd postponed it due to the recent funeral, which had the entire town in attendance.

"She fits in nicely."

Noah didn't have to ask who his dad was referring to in his random declaration to no one in particular.

"It's not like that, Dad." Noah couldn't stop his thoughts from drifting back to the first moment he'd caught sight of Reese. He'd told himself as she walked through the woods and away from his property that he should keep his distance. He hadn't realized just how much of a significance those words held until now. "She's got a life back in Springfield. We're enjoying each other's company while she's here, and we both have an understanding. That's all."

"Has there been any other attempts to warn her to leave town?"

"I know where you're going with that topic, and you can stop. You already know the answer to your question." Noah ran a hand over his face in frustration. It was his mother who used to interfere with his personal life. Not his dad. "I still come home from time to time to get clothes."

The past week had passed as if it were any other summer in Blyth Lake. No one had made an attempt to threaten Reese or harm her in any other way. There was still a foreboding air hanging around town ever since Deputy Wallace's murder, which was the town's current top subject matter.

"Look, it's not like you're seventeen years old," Gus pointed out with a bit of humor only he was benefiting from. "You're a grown man, and she is certainly grown, too. You can sleep with whomever you want, son."

Reese mentioned she'd drive over to the diner to pick up some sandwiches, but maybe they were better off cleaning up and going together. Then again, his father might continue this conversation later today as if it had never ended. It was better to take care of this now.

"I like her, Dad. I like her a lot." Well, those words weren't what he'd wanted to say. Noah shot a glance toward the open doorway. "It's only been around two weeks since I met her. I can't be asking her opinion on curtains, flooring, or furniture. This is my house. She won't even be around to see the finished product, though I wish she would be."

"Did I ever tell you about the time I met your mother?" Gus

folded his arms over his chest and settled in with a smile of remembrance on his rugged face. "Birdie would host these movie nights at the lake once a week back when your mother and I were in high school. I was painting the plywood projection screen to make some money on the side, and up walked the most beautiful woman I had ever laid eyes on. And there I was, covered in white paint. I looked like an idiot."

Noah had heard this story before, but it had always been in his mother's point of view. He didn't know that his dad had been working that day for Birdie. His mom made it sound as if they'd shown up with separate groups of friends when she approached him on a dare.

"My Mary rested her hands on my shoulders and planted a kiss on my right cheek, which was the only spot I hadn't gotten paint on me. She told me I was taking her to the ice cream parlor after the movie that night." Gus shook his head in wonderment, his thoughts lost back in time. "I knew better than to argue with a girl as pretty as her, so I spent my whole paycheck I'd earned that day buying both of us a root beer float that very night. She looked me straight in the eyes over that checkered tablecloth and told me that her bridesmaid dresses were going to be the same color blue as my eyes."

Noah could still picture his mother laughing as she told that very same story every year on their anniversary. She would fan herself with her hand, as if she couldn't believe she'd been so bold as to make such a declaration.

"What I'm saying, son, is that time doesn't matter as much as you might think. One day, one month, or one year doesn't change when two people are meant to be with one another." Gus cleared his throat, almost as if he realized how sentimental he sounded about love. There was also a sadness that the years hadn't erased at losing the woman he loved more than life itself.

"All I'm saying is don't let something this good slip between your fingers because of how it may look to anyone other than you two."

"Hey," Reese called out a little breathlessly as she leaned around the doorway with a smile on her face. "I'm heading into town to pick up lunch. Is there anything else you two need?"

"Maybe I should head into town with you," Noah suggested, not so much to get away from the conversation with his dad anymore, but because of the reminder that the man who'd threatened her was still out there somewhere.

"Don't be silly. I can always take my scatter gun." Reese tossed another smile over her shoulder when the purr of an engine came to life. Her gaze softened in understanding when she turned back around. "I'm following Tiny and Rose into town. Besides, nothing else has happened recently."

That was the problem. A predator would sometimes allow its prey to have a sense of false security right before it dealt its final blow. Were they being lulled into a false sense of security or had the perpetrator left town?

Noah's cell phone chimed, giving Reese a chance to wiggle her fingers and disappear before he could stop her.

"Detective, what can I do for you?" Noah stood as he took the call, brushing off the dust that had accumulated on his jeans. "Have the DNA results come in?"

"We're still waiting on the lab, but I thought you and Ms. Woodward should know that I did a little digging into Sophia Morton's disappearance."

"Can you hold on a moment?" Noah quickly crossed the bare floor in an effort to stop Reese. She should hear whatever was about to be revealed. Unfortunately, she'd already hopped into the cab of his truck and was pulling out of the driveway. "Um, sorry. What were you saying?"

"I took the information Reese gave me in regards to Sophia and did a little asking around." The background noise of ringing phones and low murmurs of conversation became somewhat louder as Detective Kendrick must have put Noah on speakerphone. "Give me a minute. I had the folder right here. Steve, did you take those files off my desk?"

Noah gestured for his father to come closer, lowering his phone so that he could also put the call on speakerphone. It was easier than having to explain this call more than once, which is what he would have to do with Reese.

"Okay. This is what I've found so far, but I wanted verification before I called Ms. Woodward."

"Verification of what?" Noah asked, confused as to why his opinion would matter in anything related to Sophia seeing as he hadn't known her.

"Well, seeing as I can't get ahold of your brother, you're going to have to do for now," Detective Kendrick shared before getting to the heart of the matter. "I've come to find out that Sophia Morton had a crush on your younger brother. The two of them were pretty close by the time camp ended."

Noah and his father stared at each other in confusion.

"Detective Kendrick, you must be mistaken." Noah shifted his weight and switched the cell phone into his left hand as he ran his fingers through his hair in bewilderment. "Lance was never involved with Sophia Morton. He would have said something to me or one of our other brothers at the time."

"You're right," Detective Kendrick agreed, though it was obvious there was a *but* somewhere in that concord. "He would have said something to you had he wanted you to know, but he didn't because Sophia asked him to keep their relationship under wraps. It had something to do with the fact that her brother was there, and she didn't want him saying anything to their father."

"If no one knew of this so-called relationship my brother had with Sophia Morton, then how do you know all of this?"

"Because your brother, Lance Kendall, was the one who drove Sophia into town to talk to Anastasia Osburn." The pause over the line signified Kendrick wasn't done dropping bombshells. "Not only did he sneak Sophia out of camp, but Emma Irwin tagged along to the meeting that night in your brother's car."

CHAPTER NINETEEN

REESE WAVED A hand out the window of Noah's truck as Rose and Tiny continued down Main Street toward the Cavern. The two of them had been checking on her every day since she'd been attacked last week, though their concern was unnecessary.

They had apparently taken it upon themselves to protect her, because they had hosted her in Blyth Lake. In some small towns, that still meant something. Responsibility wasn't something one delegated to another. That had been how she was raised, and it was true here in Noah's hometown as well.

What had everybody on the edge of their seats was the fact that nothing else had happened that would indicate she was still in danger. Had the threat passed or was the monster lying in wait? Was he biding his time until another opportunity arose to perpetrate his next attack?

Disturbingly enough, time had slipped by. Everything had gotten back to normal ever since Deputy Wallace's murder. It made her wonder if the killer was only lying low until the state police backed off the investigation, or did he or she complete what he or she had set out to do?

Reese had mentioned that fact to Detective Kendrick the other day on the phone, but he said that he could find no link connecting Deputy Wallace to Emma Irwin, Sophia, or herself. It was frustrating, but yet this past week had also been one of the best experiences she'd ever had in her life in the form of Noah.

Noah Kendall had swept her off her feet. She hadn't meant to fall for him the way she had. If she were given any power, it would be to stop time so that this summer break would last forever. She suspected that many summer lovers wished for exactly the same thing, but none of them had kept that second hand from sweeping away the seconds until there were no more to be had.

"You're going to get heat stroke if you stay inside that truck any longer."

Calvin was staring at her strangely as he stood in front of the diner with his hand on the silver handle. Reese hadn't realized how much time had passed since she'd shut off the engine. This was what Noah did to her...he made her lose any sense of time.

The summer was eventually going to end, and she would have to go back to her life in Springfield where she was all alone once again.

"You caught me, Calvin." Reese brushed aside her melancholy about what the next month held for her as she stepped out of the truck. She smiled at him as he held the door open for her to enter. "Were the fish biting this morning?"

"No, damn it," Calvin grumbled, taking off his baseball cap as he walked to his usual stool at the counter. "It's too damn hot. I got out there too late in the morning. Someone had chores for me to do."

"We're due for some rain," Harlan said after Molly refilled his iced tea. "I'm just hoping it holds off until after the open house on Sunday. I put a lot of money into advertising for the Langston property. I'd hate to see it wasted."

"Oh, great. A cold weather front will push the fishing out for a few days."

"What can I get you, doll?" Molly took the pencil from behind her ear and set the tip to her pad while she ignored all the drama.

"Three BLTs with steak fries, please," Reese ordered before following up with a request of three slices of apple pie for dessert. "And I'll take mine with a coffee while I wait, if you don't mind."

"You got it." Molly ripped the small green piece of paper out of her pad before sliding it underneath a clip on the rotating aluminum ring. "Order up!"

Reese made her way to the booth she usually sat in when she came by herself, though she and Noah had rarely left her house this past week without one another. He'd brought over a small grill from his dad's place. They'd had barbeque chicken, steaks, and even some brats. They'd gone to the small grocery store and stocked up for the week. That reminded her that she and Noah would need to make a trip back into town tomorrow.

"You're settling in rather nicely, aren't you?"

Reese grimaced when she realized that Whitney was sitting at the table across from the booth she'd chosen. The blonde woman didn't have the most welcoming demeanor, and her intentions toward Noah were obvious.

"Oh, I'm just here for the summer." Reese unraveled the napkin that was on the table and took out the fork. She wished Molly would hurry up with that pie. "But Blyth Lake is such a beautiful town."

"That's an odd thing to say after discovering a body, being attacked, and being the one to call 911 because Deputy Wallace was murdered." Whitney was obviously done with her lunch, but she hadn't eaten alone. There were two empty plates, along with two used glasses. What was keeping her here? "I would have left town a long time ago."

"You still can," Cassie quipped from the booth in front of

Reese. She was doing paperwork, but apparently hadn't missed the unwanted exchange. "No one is standing in your way, Whitney."

"Humorous as ever," Whitney replied wryly, snatching her purse off the back of her chair. "I'm just saying that trouble seems to follow poor little Reese around this town."

"We all knew what you were saying. You aren't that hard to read." Cassie looked at Reese and lifted an eyebrow in commiseration. "How's the job search coming along, Whitney?"

Reese really didn't know Whitney's background, other than the woman had come back home to take care of her dad. Regardless of the fact that her objective was probably to get Noah Kendall into her bed and then to wed, Whitney was due some credit for being there when health issues affected her family.

"You ready?" The question was asked by an older gentleman who had walked over from the restrooms on the other side of the diner. He was a bit out of breath, and his sunken cheekbones told of his ailing health. "You can drop me off at the Cavern. I'll see if they need any help getting ready for tonight's celebration."

Her heart ached for the sorrow etched across Whitney's face as she stared at her father with dying hopes that he would change his mind. Noah had mentioned that Jeremy Bell had a problem with alcohol. It didn't look as if the man had any intention of giving it up in the last few years of his life.

Reese was surprised when his dark gaze landed on her, preventing Whitney from heading toward the exit. She even rested a hand on her father's arm to stop him from engaging in conversation, but he shook her off.

"Are you that woman going around town asking questions about Sophia Morton?" The diner instantly fell silent, waiting for Reese to answer. She shifted uncomfortably in her seat as he looked her up and down with interest. "I helped out at the camp that summer, you know. She was a very pretty girl and everyone knew her, regardless of what they might say now."

Reese swallowed down the bile that had hit the back of her throat as his words indicated a familiar knowledge of her cousin. She'd never set down her fork, so she was able to grip the silverware rather than lash out in anger.

"Yes, I'm Sophia's cousin." Reese cleared her throat and dove headfirst into her initial reason for visiting Blyth Lake. "She went missing a year after Emma. I thought there may be a connection. Do you recall anything that might help me in my search for her?"

All eyes were now riveted to Jeremy Bell, who pulled out a pack of cigarettes from the pocket on the front of his shirt. Whitney thinned her lips and took them out of his hand when he was about to take one out of the package.

"Other than telling you that Sophia was able to help Emma learn how to swim, I don't know what else I could tell you." Jeremy looked around the diner, catching sight of Calvin and Harlan sitting at the counter. He licked his top teeth before calling out one of the patrons. "Calvin, you remember that pretty brunette who hung around Emma, don't you?"

"I've already spoken with Reese," Calvin shared, never turning around to join the discussion.

"Hmmm, I don't think you hung out with those girls much, did you, Whitney?" Jeremy eyed his daughter, who stood a good six inches shorter.

"No," Whitney replied with a tight smile. It was obvious she didn't know how to extricate her dad from this uncomfortable conversation. "Their cabin was on the other side of the property from where I was staying. Dad, we really should go."

Jeremy surprised everyone when he took a few steps forward, placing his hands on the laminate table right in front of Reese. She was so surprised at his sudden movement that she didn't have time to lean back.

Jeremy Bell whispered something in her ear that she initially thought she'd misheard. No one had ever given her any indication that what he was saying was factual. It wasn't until he pulled away that she witnessed a softening in his expression that he'd not allowed anyone to witness.

He catered to the town's opinion of him, but there was an underlying decency he concealed from those who had hidden agendas…such as his manipulating daughter.

"Good luck to you, Ms. Woodward."

It was obvious to her that everyone wanted to know what he'd whispered in her ear, especially Whitney. She hesitated before following him out the door.

"Reese?" Cassie's gaze lingered on the door as the Bells exited, as did everyone else's. It wasn't long before all eyes were on Reese. The reverberation of the bell overhead was the only sound carrying through the diner. "What was that about?"

"I'm not sure," Reese answered honestly in a hesitant tone, not willing to share something so unsubstantiated. She really needed to talk to Noah. She suddenly had the urge to be in the protection of his arms. "Um, Molly? Could I have those pies to go, after all?"

CHAPTER TWENTY

NOAH TEXTED A lengthy message to Lance, figuring his baby brother would eventually be able to reach out and explain the contextual bomb Detective Kendrick had dropped on the phone.

"Lance would have said something twelve years ago if whatever he and those girls had done that night had anything to do with either disappearance, of that I'm sure." Gus took out his trusty handkerchief and dabbed the perspiration off his forehead. They'd moved outside to the shade of the large oak tree in the front yard to wait for Reese's return. "Your mother and I raised you boys better than to keep something so important from the police."

Gus wasn't going to get an argument from his son. Noah agreed wholeheartedly that if anything illegal or illicit had occurred that particular night, Lance would have said something to one of his brothers or their parents. He was stateside, so getting ahold of him shouldn't have been an issue. Why wasn't he responding to Detective Kendrick's calls?

"Lance is due home in a few weeks on terminal leave, but I'm sure he'll call me back today." Noah looked over toward the woods where the shortcut was located, finally recognizing the shitstorm they'd unraveled when he and Reese had taken a sledgehammer to one of the walls. "When you think about it, Lance was seeing Brynn by the time winter rolled around that year. Whatever relationship or crush Lance and Sophia may have had on one another faded after that summer was over. Plus, he wouldn't have known she ever went missing a year later. He was getting ready to finish school and head off to boot camp, remember?"

"It still doesn't explain why Lance would have risked the grounding of his young life to sneak two girls out of Birdie's camp." Gus had taken a large bucket of scrap wood they'd emptied into the bed of his truck and turned it over to use as a seat in the front yard. The porch still had some decaying planks that needed to be replaced. "You know how strict Birdie was with those overnight campers."

The sound of his truck finally broke through the trees. It wasn't long before she pulled up close to the porch. He only had to look at her pretty face through the windshield to know something had happened while she was in town.

Noah had his hand on the driver's side door before her white flip-flop ever hit the ground.

"Are you okay?"

Reese didn't answer, but his chest tightened when her bottom lip tremored. He instinctively wrapped his arms around her as she stepped into his embrace. Whatever had happened was more emotional than it was physical. He breathed a sigh of relief to know she hadn't been attacked again.

"Reese," Noah murmured reassuringly as he took her by the shoulders and pushed her back just enough so that he could see her expression. "What happened?"

"Jeremy and Whitney Bell were at the diner when I was picking up lunch." Reese brushed back a flyaway strand, showing him her troubled gaze. Those beautiful brown eyes of hers were heavy with confusion. "At first, I had terrible visions of him doing something horrible to Sophia. He was acting so strange.

But then he leaned down and whispered something in my ear so that no one else could hear what he was telling me."

For the life of him, he couldn't figure out what Jeremy Bell had to do with Sophia or Emma. It wasn't like Whitney had ever hung out with Emma, unless she tagged along with her older sister. Was that the connection? Had Shae Irwin told Whitney something that would give an explanation as to why Emma had disappeared?

"Noah, Jeremy Bell said that I might want to talk to Annie about what she and Sophia *really* talked about that night." Reese wiped the moisture away that had gathered underneath her lashes. "I knew there was something else to that conversation. I knew it. When we talked to Annie last week, it didn't make any sense that Sophia would seek her out because she'd uncovered that Annie was actually Anastasia Pearl Osburn. There had to be more to the story."

Noah didn't like all of these loose ends, either. A lot of this responsibility had been on Sheriff Percy to help the state with their investigation. Towns of this size were close-knit, which is where the sheriff could have used his influence to seek out the truth. Unfortunately, the sheriff was all but retired on active duty. He didn't want to do anything that might upset the applecart.

Was Emma's time at camp related to the reason she vanished all those years ago? It was highly doubtful, but it was still a lead that should have been checked out by law enforcement.

"There's something else." Noah didn't want to add to Reese's stress, but he couldn't withhold the information Detective Kendrick had given over the phone. "The night that Sophia went to see Annie? My younger brother was the one who snuck her out of camp and drove them over to her place."

Noah shifted backward, giving Reese room to step away

from his truck. He shut the door behind her, leaving the food in the back seat for now. She leaned against the hot metal as she absorbed this latest bit of news. She was taking this better than he would have thought.

"How do you know this?"

"Detective Kendrick called right as you were heading into town."

"And you didn't know? Lance never said anything to you about that?" Reese glanced past his shoulder to where Gus was waiting patiently. She'd gotten to know him this past week, so Noah wasn't surprised that she was worried about hurting his feelings. "Can we call him? Can you reach out to him? We need to know what was actually said that night."

"I've already sent him a text message to call me back." Noah didn't like to make excuses for his siblings. They'd been taught honor at a very young age. Even with that lesson, people made mistakes. "He's returning home in a few weeks for good, so I know he's stateside. It shouldn't be long before I hear something back from him."

Noah prayed that he was right, because he couldn't fathom his brother evading a police investigation.

He was surprised when Reese quickly spun around, opening the door to the truck. She retrieved the bags with the Styrofoam containers inside of them, hooking one on her arm and carrying the other two with her right hand. With a bump of her hip, she closed the door. The pace in which she did so set him on edge, because he could already tell what she had in mind.

"Reese, we should call Detective Kendrick to let him know what Jeremy Bell said to you today." Couldn't she see that they were stepping on a hornet's nest? "Let Kendrick talk to him to find out what he knows."

"Why wait when we can drive to Annie's house and talk to

her?" Reese reasoned, slipping around him and heading toward Gus. He instinctively stood and took the food from her hands, shooting a commiserating look toward Noah. He'd seen it a million times when his mother had become headstrong about a subject she became determined to sort out. "Do you know where she lives? If not, we can stop back at the diner in town and get the address from Cassie."

"Of course, I know where Annie lives, Reese," Noah said, bringing her up short when she would have walked right back to his vehicle. He rested his hands on her arms to try and get her to see reason. "One week ago, you were attacked in a public place. Someone didn't want you asking questions, and he or she went to pretty disturbing lengths to get his or her point across. It's not smart to be traipsing around town when whoever it was who tried to hurt you is still out there free."

"And you think it's Annie?" Reese had her oversized brown sunglasses on top of her head, but she lowered them onto the bridge of her nose to make her point. She was going to question Annie with or without him. "She's an eighty-some-year-old woman, Noah. Trust me, she wasn't the one who attacked me in that restroom."

"I never said that I believed Annie was responsible for what happened to you, but you've been asking questions that someone is uncomfortable with when it comes to Emma and Sophia." Noah could tell by the look on Reese's face that he was going to lose this battle. A glance toward his father sitting on that damned bucket and eating his club sandwich as if he were watching a fucking television show proved that he wasn't going to be any help. "Am I the only one who sees the sense in calling Detective Kendrick to take care of this?"

"You're the only one I see standing in my way, at the moment," Reese pointed out, shooing her fingers at him like he was a field mouse caught in her kitchen. "Annie basically sought me out last time, so she's already proved she's willing to talk to me. I can get answers quicker than Detective Kendrick can, and you know it."

Reese brushed past Noah, causing his arms to drop to his side. He lifted them up in frustration, but his father only took another bite of his sandwich as he settled in to enjoy his lunch and this impromptu skit from daytime television.

Son of a bitch.

"Are you coming?"

"I'm driving." Noah needed to be in control of something. If that something was his own truck, then so be it. Reese had already settled herself into the passenger side of his F150, dangling his keys in her hand. "Have you considered calling Tanner and asking him about this new development?"

"Tanner?" Reese practically laughed in mockery over her cousin's name. "I'm barely speaking to him right now. The reason he attended camp that year was to keep an eye on Sophia, because my uncle never let her do anything alone. And what did Tanner do that he decided wasn't of importance? He was too busy trying to impress some girl named Beth Ann Mason to check on his sister or do what he'd been sent there to do. He said he only saw her twice, and that was when Birdie called camp meetings."

Noah didn't think it was a good idea to bring up that Beth Ann had been his first kiss. He might not be the smartest man in Blyth Lake, but he sure as hell was not totally devoid of common sense.

"Dad, can you go ahead and lock up?" Noah asked through his open window. He had finally accepted the inevitable. "I think we might be awhile."

Gus raised a hand in acknowledgement as he continued to

eat his lunch, smiling after his son. Noah's stomach growled, but it looked as if he wasn't going to be eating anything till supper time.

Noah didn't utter a word until he pulled the truck into her driveway, shutting off the engine before she could protest.

"If we're going to go traipsing around town, please allow me to have a shower and change my clothes." Noah opened the driver's side door before walking around the front bumper and assisting her down from the cab. Her eyes were still covered by those oversized sunglasses, but her scrunched up nose at the delay was too cute to resist. He leaned in and kissed her forehead before jogging up the steps and using the key she'd given him days ago. It wasn't like there was any significance in the gesture, and he certainly didn't put a spin on it. "Give me ten."

"Eight," Reese called out with a smile. No one else, besides probably her family, would have caught the strained line running across her forehead as she worried about what they were about to uncover. "You could earn a real kiss if you're ready in five."

"You're on."

Noah quickly made his way through the living room, down the short hallway, and into the bedroom. His open duffel bag still sat on the chair in the corner, and his toothbrush was still seated beside hers in the ceramic holder.

This was a temporary situation.

Reese had come here looking for answers, and today might be the day she got what she wanted. That left Noah wondering if she wouldn't cut short this so-called vacation and head home once she'd found those answers.

He tossed his clothes into the hamper next to the dresser with a little more force than necessary and made his way into the bathroom. With a flick of the handle, the shower came to life. He rested his palms against the counter and stared at himself in the mirror.

It shouldn't matter when Reese went back to her life.

He'd gone into this summer fling with his eyes wide open.

Then why did thinking about her leaving feel as though a knife was piercing his chest?

CHAPTER TWENTY-ONE

"THIS ISN'T AT all what I expected." Reese was standing next to Noah in front of his truck, both of them staring in awe at the ten or so chickens pecking the ground in front of a two-story house painted sky blue with a porch covering two sides. It was absolutely stunning. "I didn't know she had that kind of money, not that I mean anything by that."

"Trust me, you and I are on the same page." Noah rested a hand on her lower back as he guided her toward the overzealous chickens. "Let's just say this place has had a major makeover since the last time I drove out this way."

Reese figured that was when Noah was a teenager. She would have kept walking had a chicken not started to flap her wings in panic when they tried to pass her.

"Oh!" Reese almost tripped Noah in her haste to avoid being attacked by militant poultry. Wouldn't that be a story tell her parents? "Shoo. Go away. Get, now."

"You grew up thirty miles from here," Noah said with a laugh. He grabbed her hand and pulled her closer to him. They finally made it to the wooden steps. "How could you be afraid of a chicken?"

"Chickens. You forgot the S. I grew up in a regular neighborhood," Reese reminded him with a little shove to his ribcage. "We didn't have any chickens. You know…houses, trees, streets, sidewalks. We didn't have any pigs, cows, or chickens."

"You didn't go to the county fair every summer like the rest of us poor country folk?" Noah knocked on the screen door. Reese noted how solid it was compared to the one on her rental house. "My brothers and I went every year, but it was Gwen who could ride horses like she was born in the saddle."

"Really? You grew up on a good-sized lot of land. I'm surprised your parents didn't—"

"Noah? Reese?" Annie didn't hesitate to open the door for them, stepping back so they could join her inside the cool interior. Reese only ever felt refreshed like this when she ate at the diner. She did her best not to moan in pleasure as they left the humidity outside. "Come in, come in. I was just about to have a glass of lemonade Cassie made this morning."

Reese's mouth began to water at the mention of the home-made beverage that contained just the right amount of sugar. It was also a good reason to delay the inevitable. Something held Reese back from asking Annie about Sophia right away for fear she would receive an answer she didn't want to hear.

It was doubtful this sweet old lady had anything to do with Sophia going missing, other than maybe giving her some details on who to contact once she arrived in Hollywood. Reese still didn't believe Sophia had gone across the country without saying a word to her family.

"What brings you two out my way? Had I known, I would have had you stop by the pharmacy to pick up my new prescription. Cassie couldn't get away from the diner this afternoon since Molly had to leave early for some reason or another. I had to have Darcy head back into town even though we'd just come through a couple of hours ago."

Annie bustled around the kitchen pouring the drinks and arranging what looked like homemade chocolate chip cookies on a sunflower plate. Her energy was high, and Reese could just imagine how hard it had been for this woman to give up her livelihood…not only once, but twice.

"Are you two going to answer my question or leave me to fill in the blanks?"

"Um, well, something's been brought to my attention that I'm hoping you can clarify," Reese explained, wrapping her hands around the cold crystal. She was used to condensation immediately coating the outside of a glass, so it was nice to allow the coolness to seep into her palms without the moisture. "I ran into Jeremy Bell at the diner today. He indicated that the talk you and Sophia had involved more than her just wanting your advice on acting."

Reese paused so she could study Annie's expression, but the older woman gave little away as she cocked a brow in question.

"We also discovered that Lance and Emma were with Sophia that night when she came to see you," Noah interjected, laying all their cards on the table. It wasn't as if this was a game where that mattered, but it did leave Reese without much wiggle room. "Reese has waited a long time to get answers regarding her cousin's disappearance. If you know something, Ms. Osburn, please tell us."

Annie sighed in resignation as she lowered her eyes to the trim on her sleeve. She was wearing a lightweight blouse, though the sleeves went to her wrists. There was no reason she needed to worry about overheating while staying inside the central air.

Reese's stomach seemed unsettled in anticipation of what the older woman was about to share with them. Jeremy Bell had been right about there being more to the story.

"Your Sophia recognized me one day when I had been visiting Cassie up at the camp. She was volunteering that year, and she needed something from the house." It was obvious that Annie was trying to remember what that something had been, but she was struggling with her memories. She batted the air with her hand in frustration. "Anyway, as I've already told you, Sophia showed up at the diner that night asking questions about my time in Hollywood. The only thing I left out is that she somehow discovered old pictures of me that I would have rather had left buried."

It took a minute for the meaning behind Annie's words to sink in.

Old pictures?

Noah cleared his throat, obviously caught off guard with the direction this conversation was going.

"Ms. Osburn, you aren't trying to say that Sophia tried to blackmail you, are you?" Reese couldn't imagine her cousin doing such a thing, even at that young of an age when common sense wasn't so common. "She—"

"Oh, no, no, no," Annie denied emphatically, waving her weathered hand in the air once more. "I didn't mean to imply that she had done anything of the sort. It came up in conversation, is all. I admit to being quite shocked she'd found something I thought had been concealed from prying eyes locally, at least. I wouldn't discuss it with her, and I won't discuss it now. It was a part of my life I'd rather forget, and at the time it could have hurt my reputation, my family, and my business. I'd like it kept quiet now, as well."

Annie took a sip of her lemonade and then carefully set her glass back down on the table. She'd straightened her shoulders, as if she was prepared to battle Reese in how the rest of the discussion was carried out. Annie believed her reputation was at stake, and it wasn't Reese's intention to upset the older woman.

Unfortunately, nothing was making any sense.

"Ms. Osburn, did this conversation happen at the diner during business hours?"

"Yes," Annie answered, though she was frowning in her attempt to recall that night. "Yes, it did. Sophia left after I'd written down on a piece of paper the agency I'd used to get my start in the movies. The reputable one, mind you. I would never in a million years dream of allowing someone as sweet as Sophia to wade through the sewer that represents the darker side of that life."

Is that what Jeremy Bell had heard that night, believing by mistake that Sophia had tried to blackmail Annie? Was he saying that he thought Annie was responsible for what could have happened to Sophia because of that destructive secret?

Or had Emma taken it upon herself do something later that was of a malicious nature?

"Did you see Emma Irwin with Sophia that night?" Noah asked, his line of thought parallel to hers. "Or my brother?"

Reese was somewhat shocked, because she hadn't figured Lance into the equation. If Sophia and Emma had somehow come up with a plan and it was the reason for their disappearances, then why leave Lance alone?

It made Reese realize how futile this visit had been.

"No, not that I recall." Annie rested her arthritic fingers to her thinned lips and shook her head. "I never questioned how she got to the diner, nor did I tell Birdie that the girl had snuck out of camp. Hollywood can be very seductive and calls out to a lot of pretty girls. It was obvious that Sophia had stars in her eyes. My heart broke when I'd heard why you were in town."

Reese sat back in somewhat defeat, realizing that none of her original speculations had any legs to stand on. Sophia visiting with Annie was nothing more than teenage dreams and wishes for a different life. Lance and Emma helping her make that happen was most likely a coincidence, especially since nothing bad had ever happened to Noah's brother.

"Thank you for talking to us today, Ms. Osburn." Noah pushed back his chair before reaching over and patting the woman's hand. She returned the gesture and squeezed his fingers when he reassured her that they wouldn't tell a soul about what Sophia had uncovered back then. Annie's private life was her own and none of anyone's business then or now. "I hope your new prescription works out. I know how hard it was for my dad to find the right medication to control his blood pressure."

"Old age isn't for the weary now, is it?"

Reese stood, though she was at a loss for words. Her mental and emotional state had been drained of the initial burst of energy from this morning. Jeremy Bell had been trying to help, and in doing so, gotten her hopes up for those elusive answers.

"I'm truly sorry that I couldn't help you more, dear," Annie said as she slowly walked them to the front door. Noah stepped out onto the porch first, but Reese hadn't braced herself for the humidity quite yet. "I do hope you find the answers you're seeking."

"Me, too," Reese murmured, taking Noah's offered hand. She winced when the oppressive heat blanketed her body once again.

Not even the chickens flapping their wings at another disruption bothered Reese as she walked to Noah's truck. She looked back over her shoulder, but Annie had already closed her front door and gone back inside to enjoy her central air.

"I'm sorry you didn't find the answers you were looking for, sweetheart." Noah lifted the handle on the passenger side door and used it to lean against as he seemed in no hurry to leave. He had a way about him that made a woman feel as if she were the only one in the world. "We'll keep looking."

"You know, I talked to every single person in my neighborhood the week Sophia went missing." Reese rested a hand on her chest as those painful memories resurfaced. "It didn't take much to convince Aunt Lydia that Sophia had run away. She'd always been one to rebel, but she never would have hurt her family in that way. I don't understand why everyone was so eager to accept that answer."

"Because it gave them hope that one day she would come back." Noah reached out and wrapped his hand around her wrist, pulling her close. He held her against him in a comforting embrace, despite the humidity. "Hope is what has us getting up every morning. Without hope, there would be no reason to go on."

"I didn't choose hope, though." Reese leaned back to see what his opinion was on the fact that she'd gone down a different road. For some reason, his outlook on such a decision was important to her. "I know she's gone, Noah. I just want answers and maybe to find whoever was responsible."

"You're a realist, sweetheart. There's nothing wrong with acceptance, either. You're misunderstanding my words. You want closure. That's healthy, but you're walking a very fine line of being dragged over into *her* life. Remember, you still have your own life to live."

Reese closed her eyes and rested her cheek on his chest, soaking in his strength. There was a truth in what he was saying, but he didn't realize just how much truth.

She did have a life back in Springfield, but she also wanted what she was creating here…with him. She wasn't so sure she wanted to leave Blyth Lake behind and all it had to offer.

CHAPTER TWENTY-TWO

"**Y**OU KNOW WHAT we need?" Noah pushed aside his empty plate and rested a hand over his full stomach. He hadn't had the meatloaf special since he'd been home last, and the effects of homestyle comfort food hadn't changed. He could go home and sleep off this food coma for the rest of the night. He wouldn't, though, not when there were more important matters at stake—like Reese's mental state. He didn't like seeing her struggle with her lack of closure. "We need a night out."

"A night out?"

At least he'd caught her attention. Her brown eyes lifted from the pecan pie that Cassie had made with a new ingredient. The entire diner had been sworn to secrecy so that Annie didn't find out that one more of her staple recipes had been altered. The only reason the patrons agreed was because the pie literally melted in their mouths.

"Yeah," Noah said encouragingly, forcing himself to lean forward in enthusiasm. He ignored the protest of his full stomach. "We spent the morning working our butts off at the house, spent most of the afternoon talking to Annie, and then taking a drive up to the lake to talk to Rose. I think we deserve a night to disconnect. We need to have some fun."

"Isn't that what we have every night?" Reese asked, wiggling her eyebrows with a smile. He fell for her a little more. "I'm rather partial to that kind of fun."

Noah was still laughing when Cassie came out from behind the counter. She was covering Molly's shift, even though she was also baking in the kitchen. It wasn't unusual for her to be somewhat quiet when she was overworked, but tonight she'd been unusually so. He was surprised when she made her way over to their table.

"Reese?" Cassie made sure her back was turned when she addressed them. "Mama called the diner earlier. She told me about your visit today, and I just want to thank you for keeping...well, you know...keeping it quiet and not telling everyone around town about what your cousin found."

Reese shared a surprised look with Noah. Cassie had known about the nude photographs? This was an unexpected turn, because that could mean someone had misunderstood Sophia's intention.

"The majority of this town are very supportive, but there's always that ten percent who can cause hate and discontent. Well, you've seen it." Cassie appeared to study the blue dishtowel intently that she was currently wringing with her hands. "My mother had come back home in order to raise me where she had family roots. It was hard enough that she'd returned with a daughter in tow without ever naming my father, but to add on the indiscretion of...those photos? Well, people tend to get rather judgmental around these parts."

Reese laid her hand over Cassie's, stilling her nervous motion. She leaned in so no one could hear her reply.

"Cassie, it wasn't my intention to come to town and expose your mother's secrets. I only wanted to find out if there was a connection between my cousin and Emma Irwin. They were attached at the hip for an entire week, and yet they never spoke to one another again. That seemed rather strange to me." Reese shook her head in regret. "I thought maybe your mother might have some answers, but it was only Sophia who walked into the diner. Noah and I can only guess that Emma and Lance didn't want anyone spotting them here, because they would have gotten caught by Birdie or their parents for sneaking out of their cabin that night."

"Well, I appreciate your discretion."

Cassie seemed to want to say more, but Uncle Jimmy chose that moment to enter the diner. She feigned her reasoning for being at their table by slipping their check underneath Noah's glass.

"You two heading over to Tiny's Cavern?" Cassie asked, raising her tone to a normal level. "Brynn is officially getting the keys tonight."

"I was just about to suggest that to Reese." Noah removed his wallet from his back pocket, taking out the appropriate amount of cash that would cover the bill and a hefty tip. He glanced across the table toward Reese. "What do you say we join in the festivities? I'll even let you beat me at pool."

"Oh, really?" Reese smiled, letting that precious dimple show he loved so much. "Ten dollars say I can take you."

"You're on, wild one." Noah pushed back his chair and stood, not expecting his uncle to call him over to the counter. "Reese, let me go and speak to my uncle. I won't be long."

"You've had an exciting return home," Uncle Jimmy said, motioning for Cassie to pour him a cup of coffee. "I thought maybe we could get together for dinner one night. You know, talk about old times."

"That'd be nice, Uncle Jimmy." Noah half-leaned on the stool, not expecting this conversation to take too long. There hadn't been a time when he'd visited home where his uncle didn't extend this same invitation over and over. Noah always accepted, yet the meal never materialized. "It's been a while since we've sat down and talked."

Jimmy not so casually looked around the diner to see who was present before leaning in close to share something he obviously regarded as important.

"I know what I saw that night. Emma Irwin was alive when she walked out of those woods."

Uncle Jimmy had barely whispered the words, but he might as well have shouted them through the rooftop. Noah had never once considered a family member might be responsible for something so evil. Had they all been fooled because the man liked to drink a little too much?

"Uncle Jimmy, maybe you should talk to—"

"Sheriff Percy?" Jimmy laughed at the suggestion, casting doubt on the motives of others. Noah didn't care for Percy, either, and he certainly hadn't been very helpful these past couple of weeks. Was there a specific reason as to why he'd been that way? "I wouldn't trust that man for all the money in the world, and that's saying something, isn't it?"

Noah didn't miss the reference to the fact that the homes purchased for the Kendall siblings had come from Earl Lawrence Kittredge. Now wasn't the time to address old family conflicts. He stuck to the matter at hand.

"Look, we don't even know if the body found was Emma Irwin," Noah reminded his uncle, doing his best to keep this conversation between themselves. Cassie had poured Jimmy a cup of coffee before taking a call on her cell phone at the end of the counter. Calvin and Harlan had already headed over to the Cavern, so there wasn't anyone else sitting on the stools. "There hasn't been any confirmation, so it's pointless to try and guess what could have happened to Emma Irwin. And no one is saying they don't believe you about that night."

"Sometimes the words don't need to be said." Jimmy took a

sip of his coffee, giving Noah a chance to check on Reese. Her pretty brown eyes were resting solely on him, so he did his best to give her a reassuring smile. "You grew up in this town and then left before you were truly an adult. You were a child. Your view of these people might as well have been cast from the face of a damned Christmas card. You see everyone the way *you* want them to be, not for who they really are. Be careful, Noah. That's all I'm saying."

Noah wasn't quite sure what that entire conversation had been about, but he sure as hell wanted to leave the diner now. There were quite a lot of questions building up about the time he'd been away. He made a mental note to have a talk with his father tomorrow morning. Maybe Gus had some idea of what Jimmy was trying to convey about the residents of Blyth Lake.

"Oh, before you go," Jimmy said, turning the top of the stool so that he was facing Noah. The older man's blue eyes softened slightly as he shared something quite shocking. "I want you to know there are no hard feelings about the money used to purchase your property. My father was a hard son of a bitch to please. My sister, though, she loved me. I might have been cut out of Earl Kittredge's will, but don't think I didn't appreciate the monthly deposits into my bank account. Your mother was a good woman."

Noah debated on continuing this conversation, but now wasn't the time or place. His dad had never once made mention of deposits going into Jimmy's account, not that it would have made a difference. Money was the root of all evil, unless one went out of their way to make it not so.

"Take care, Uncle Jimmy."

"Is everything okay?" Reese met Noah in the middle of the diner, falling into step with him as they headed toward the door. "You don't look too happy."

"Which is why we're heading to Tiny's Cavern." Noah wasn't going to damper tonight's festivities. They both needed this fun escape. Everything else could be put on hold. "Are you ready to get your ass beat at pool?"

"Bring it on, Noah Kendall," Reese said with a smile, stepping out into the dark of night. He let the door close behind them. The street lights provided illumination, unlike the storefronts. Most of the shops had closed and a lot of the locals were most likely already at the Cavern. That didn't explain the desolation that hovered over Main Street. "I guess those storms are finally getting ready to roll in."

No sooner had Reese verbalized those ill-fated words than lightning streaked overhead. Thunder wasn't far behind. The low rumble from the increase in pressure and temperature was rather threatening.

"It sounds like it's going to be pretty bad." Noah rested a hand on her lower back and guided her across the street. He considered going back for his truck to park it closer to the Cavern two blocks down, but the skies were about to open up above them. "We need the rain, but let's hope the storms ease up to a light drizzle. That kind of lightning is known to cause forest fires and a crapload of damage."

Noah hadn't realized that Reese had stopped before she'd stepped onto the curb. His attention had been on the weather and trying to time their arrival before the rain. He caught both of them before they fell onto the sidewalk.

"Shit," Noah muttered, righting both of them as he looked down at her ankles. "Are you okay?"

"Yes, but I thought…" Whatever Reese had been going to say trailed off as she carefully and quietly searched the area behind them. Noah looked over his shoulder, but he couldn't see anything that would have caught her attention. "Never mind.

I thought I saw someone."

"Never mind?" Noah didn't want to point out all the issues and run-ins they'd had recently, nor did he want to bring up Deputy Wallace's murder. Unfortunately, he didn't have that luxury when it came to her health. "*Did* you see someone? We can always head back to your place."

"No, I don't want to do that." Reese continued to observe the shadows of the night in basically every direction, finally giving up when nothing out of the ordinary happened or came into view. She shook her head as if she could dispel her worries. "Let's go before we get soaking wet."

Noah let her get a couple steps ahead before he ventured forth, trusting her instincts. After all that had happened, she might want to believe what she'd sensed was nothing, but wishing didn't make it so.

Lightning lit up the sky once more, followed by a crack of thunder that wasn't near as smooth as the previous rumbling. He'd made it known to Reese numerous times that he wasn't a superstitious man, but that didn't mean he ignored signs that were right in front of him.

Something menacing was hanging in the air.

It was only a matter of time before it made an appearance.

CHAPTER TWENTY-THREE

"**N**OAH KENDALL WAS your first kiss, huh?" Reese asked before she tossed a peanut into her mouth to prevent Noah from seeing her smile. She raised her eyebrows in a dare, taunting him to deny what the pretty redhead at their table had just divulged with the help of her second draft beer. "You know, my cousin had a crush on you back in the day. Tanner attended summer camp two years in a row to try and garner your attention."

There was a country music band set up on a small stage in the back. The bass was loud enough that she could sense the deep-toned reverberations through the soles of her flip-flops. She and Noah had decided not to head back to the house to change clothes.

Most of the patrons were dressed casually, though some of the older residents were outfitted in their business attire. It seemed that some had come directly from work, such as Harlan and his wife.

Laughter and conversation could be heard over the upbeat tempo of a popular song. Glasses and bottles clinked together every now and then, as well as the occasional knocking of pool balls from where the bar's two tables were currently in use.

It was as if a body had never been found, nor had the murder of Deputy Wallace ever been committed. Reese wondered how his family was coping with his death while everyone carried on as if nothing evil had touched their town.

Maybe it was the residents' way of carrying on and celebrating the deputy's memory. She knew first hand that the world didn't stop spinning when hers had come to a complete stop. Life carried on.

"Tanner Morton was your cousin?" Beth Ann asked in surprise with a laugh, nudging the man beside her. Her question certainly brought Reese back to the present. "Jack, this boy would leave me flowers on my cabin doorstep every morning. I didn't figure out who it was until Julie set her alarm for some ungodly hour and sat by the window, peering through the curtains to see if she could catch whoever it was."

"Let me guess," Noah chimed in as he rested his arm across the back of Reese's chair. "You thought it was Chad Schaeffer."

Even in the dim lighting of the bar it was easy to catch the slight flush on Beth Ann's cheeks as she feigned innocence.

"I have no earthly idea what you're talking about."

Jack leaned in toward Beth Ann and pressed a kiss to her temple. His love for her was evident, and it wouldn't surprise Reese if he put a ring on Beth Ann's finger by the end of the year.

Conversations broke off into smaller groups, leaving Reese to observe old friends getting reacquainted. She hadn't grown up here and didn't know the majority of the crowd, but it was easy to distinguish who had remained close and who hadn't.

Noah had pointed out a few classmates he'd graduated with, though they stayed at their own tables minding their own business. Billy Stanton was at the bar talking with two women no one at their table seemed to know of, while Whitney danced in the corner with the same man she'd been seen with most of this week. Chad was throwing darts with a man who went by the name of Irish. She was relatively certain it was some type of nickname, but no one at her table could confirm that.

Reese was honestly surprised to see so many of the locals attend a celebration that was in name only. Brynn Mercer had signed the papers to buy this place over a month ago. Maybe tonight held a special significance that Reese wasn't aware of, but it sure had everyone involved.

Jeremy Bell sat at the bar talking sports with Miles and Gus, while Brynn Mercer stood behind the bar serving up drinks almost nonstop. Calvin, Harlan, Rose, Tiny, and Cassie were all congregated around a round table in the corner.

Harlan had brought his wife, who seemed nice enough, while Cassie had shown up less than an hour ago. She'd closed the diner early and joined in the festivities.

The only time everyone had abruptly stopped talking was when Pete Anderson had opened the door and crossed the threshold. Reese didn't think the man looked like a killer. He had a receding brown hairline and wire-rimmed glasses that didn't hide his soft demeanor. His stride wasn't mercenary, but more of a man who was determined to find answers. Everyone seemed a bit surprised when he tapped Chad on the shoulder. The two of them then grabbed a table in the far corner away from prying ears.

"Shit," Jack muttered with a shake of his head. "Vultures. Every last one of them. Can't Brynn throw them out or something?"

Them turned out to be one of the media teams that were residing in the B&B on Main Street. There were three of them total, with the lone woman being the face of the crew. They scanned the place and it wasn't long before they spotted Pete Anderson. Surprisingly, they stayed far away and proceeded to the pool table area where a group of men had laid down their sticks in favor of the dartboard Chad and Irish had vacated.

"As long as they don't cause any trouble, Brynn will take their money." Noah tilted his beer bottle back and took a swig as he monitored the situation. "Besides, Tiny is keeping an eye on them. They won't get away with anything."

Reese remained silent, rolling her right shoulder in an attempt to relieve the disturbing sensation that had settled over her. She tried to casually look around the room once more in an effort to find out who was making her uncomfortable. The hair on the back of her neck had been standing at attention for quite some time, similar to what she experienced that night in the woods when she'd caught someone watching her.

She met gazes with a few people, such as Harlan and Cassie. She even caught Pete Anderson glancing her way, but he seemed to be observing the group rather than her specifically.

"Are you okay?" Noah murmured, leaning in so that no one else could hear his question.

"Yeah," Reese assured him, tucking the strand of hair that had fallen out of her scrunchy. She wasn't about to worry him when this was the first time he'd really been able to connect with a lot of his old friends. It hadn't been until this evening that she realized how much of his time she'd monopolized. "I'm fine. I'm going to go use the restroom, though. I'll be right back."

It didn't surprise her that Noah shifted in his chair so that he could keep an eye on her as she maneuvered her way through the crowd. She'd never seen such a small area packed with so many people. Wasn't there some sort of fire code? It wouldn't surprise her if the fire marshal were in attendance, cutting Brynn Mercer a little slack due to the reasoning behind such a crowd.

"Excuse me," Reese muttered, slipping in between two parties who were immersed in their own separate conversations. "Sorry. Excuse me."

After repeating that mantra until the small hallway appeared in the back, Reese finally had a clear line of sight to the women's restroom. This direction led her straight past the small table that housed Chad Schaeffer and Pete Anderson. Irish was nowhere to be found.

It wasn't until she was a few feet away from the duo that she could see the anxiety and concern in Pete's eyes as to what had transpired in the last few weeks.

Reese didn't want to interrupt, so she nodded an acknowledgement to the men before continuing across the hardwood floor. The band started to play another song, this one even more popular, garnering cheers from the crowd. She had just finished crossing the dance area when a lot of the women had taken their positions to do some type of line dance.

It didn't take her long to enter the narrow hallway where she could no longer distinguish between the bass of the music and the rumbling thunder outside. The back door was maybe ten feet from the two restrooms sitting opposite one another. She resisted the urge to look outside to see just how bad the weather had turned, her body signaling that hearing the rain would only make her troubles worse.

"Oh!"

Reese put a hand over her heart when the door to the women's restroom opened. A pretty blonde stepped out with a friend, the two already singing along with the song. They looked to be barely twenty-one years old, and she hoped they lived in town. They had definitely had one too many.

She stepped inside the small restroom, noting that there was a stall. This allowed others to come in and wash their hands without having to wait for someone to use the toilet. Well, it was a good thing that stall was empty, because her bladder wasn't going to hold itself much longer.

Reese flipped the latch on the door to the stall, grateful to find that the restroom was kept clean. She quickly relieved herself and was buttoning her jean shorts when the outer door opened and slowly closed behind whoever had entered. Reese would have stepped out had she not heard the sink start to flow with water.

Great.

She grimaced, recalling reading once about bathroom etiquette. Had there been three stalls, one should always use the outer ones for more privacy. The situation here was vastly different, but seeing as there was only one stall, the woman who entered should have wanted to use the toilet. Instead, whoever had entered clearly only intended to wash her hands.

Should she wait here until the woman was done?

"You can come out."

Reese tilted her head back in disbelief, wondering what she'd done to deserve such a bad luck streak. She really wasn't looking forward to having another confrontation with Whitney Bell.

She sighed in resignation and flipped the lever, allowing the stall door to gradually open.

Sure enough, Whitney stood at the sink. She shut off the water and reached for the brown paper towel contraption. She pulled a few out and wiped her hands as she met Reese's gaze in the mirror.

This was not the Whitney she'd met at the beach, nor the Whitney she'd run into at the diner.

"I wanted to thank you for how you handled my dad at lunch today." Whitney dropped her gaze to the brown paper towels as she finished drying off her hands. She then tossed the remnants into the trashcan beside the sink. "He's made some mistakes in the past that he's accepted he'll never overcome. He acts a certain way, but he really has been a very good father to me."

Which would explain why Whitney had felt the need to return home. She wanted to be there for her father in his time of need. It didn't matter that she became frustrated with Jeremy Bell's inability to stop drinking or the way he carried himself around town. The bottom line was that he was her father.

Reese had misjudged the woman.

"You're welcome," Reese replied in kind, thinking all the while it was only human decency to be kind to one another. While small towns were known for their tight-knit community, there were times when too much knowledge stained their opinions. "You shouldn't worry about what others think, Whitney. I've been fighting against what people assumed about Sophia for most of my life."

Whitney nodded her understanding, but she didn't stay behind to listen to Reese's advice or share her troubles any more than she already had. The blonde exited, leaving Reese alone in the small restroom. She made her way to the sink and washed her hands, using the pink soap from the dispenser attached to the wall.

Reese glanced at herself in the mirror and decided to take her scrunchy out so she could run her fingers through her hair, trying to look somewhat decent. Noah liked it when she wore her hair down. It was almost the end of June, meaning she had less than a month here in Blyth Lake. After that, she was due to visit Heartland for a week before heading back to Springfield to get ready for another school year.

The thing of it was…she wasn't ready to leave this small town.

She wasn't ready to leave Noah.

It was getting harder and harder not to call her mother for advice. Besides Sophia, Gail Woodward was the only one who wouldn't cushion the truth.

Had Reese fallen for someone in the span of three weeks?

And what was the next step? Should she extend the invitation that he could visit her in Springfield when time allowed? Was it bad-mannered for her to invite herself back here on the weekends?

What if she was walking away from *the one?*

It wasn't as if she needed to figure it all out tonight. There was still quite a bit time between now and then. He might be the first to bring it up, offering both of them a solution. That would certainly tell her they were on the same page.

As of right now, tonight was about forgetting responsibilities. It was a celebration for the town, for Brynn Mercer, for Tiny and Rose, and even for Reese and Noah. There were moments that everyone needed a break from reality, and this was one of those times.

Reese slid her hair scrunchy into the front pocket of her shorts. She'd leave her hair down, and a shiver of excitement ran over her spine in anticipation of seeing Noah's blue eyes glisten with arousal when she finally returned to their table.

Yes, she would forget about everything tonight and just enjoy his company.

Reese opened the door, allowing the muffled sounds of the bar to become somewhat deafening. She stepped out and was about to make her way back to her table when she froze.

At the end of the hallway stood a man...the imposing man she'd seen at the beach. He had the same build as the one she'd seen in the woods that night.

And he was blocking her way back to Noah.

The man took a step forward, his words muffled by the booming bass coming from the band. At least, she thought that was why she couldn't hear him. It might also have to do with the fact that her heartrate had accelerated to the point of physical pain in her chest.

Blood rushed through her ears and perspiration instantly coated her body as she struggled with her fight or flight instinct.

Flight won out, this time around.

Reese spun around and headed for the exit. In the back of her mind, she was telling herself to take this route around to the front, where she could reach Noah. It never occurred to her that the man might reach her before she made it that far.

Her palms hit the silver bar in the middle of the door, causing her body to spill out into the night. Rain was coming down in torrents, hitting the pavement in a unified sheet of water. She was soaked to the skin before she even took one step forward.

She didn't have to look behind her to know that he'd decided to follow, closing the distance between them.

Thunder rolled across the darkened sky above while lightning streaked through the blackness. The pelting and tinging sounds of the rain striking the blacktop were diminished by the smacking of her flip flops.

"Hey!"

Reese could sense him closing in on her before she had a chance to exit the alleyway onto Main Street. His fingers slipped off her shoulder, though she wasn't sure it was due to the slickness of the rain or the fact that she forced her legs to run faster.

Her attempt at reaching Main Street came to an end when she stumbled forward due to the front of her flip flop catching on something and folding underneath her foot. She instinctively shielded the fall with her hands.

She experienced no pain as the rocks and gravel dug into the skin of her palms. All she could think of was that she couldn't allow this man to kill her in a dark alleyway during a thunderstorm. No one could hear her scream, and no one was coming to her rescue.

Reese could see the man's hands coming toward her as she flipped over so she could keep him in her line of sight. She blinked away the rain to focus, only to then have a sheet of lightning illuminate the sky above them.

"You don't—"

The crack of thunder surprised them both, but it gave her the advantage in addition to the surge of adrenaline rushing through her bloodstream. Her flip flop had come off somewhere between falling and her shifting over so that she could face him, so it was the heel of her foot that she used to bring the man to his knees.

Reese kicked him in the groin as hard as she could and then waited for her next opportunity. She then instinctively landed another kick to his jaw the second he leaned over in pain, allowing her heel to connect with his jaw.

Hell, it might have been his nose, but she was too busy trying to stand up to take stock. She hadn't even taken a step backward when the side exit of the bar flung open to reveal Noah. The street lamp provided enough clarification that she could make out his features. He was by her side before she ever said his name.

"Darcy!"

Cassie and a few of the other patrons had followed Noah outside, though it was Gus who was holding his cell phone to his ear. Everyone else looked on in shock as Cassie hovered over the man who was still huddled on the ground with blood trailing down his face.

A rage unlike anything Reese had ever experienced flooded her body, but Noah maintained his hold on her.

"Darcy? This is Darcy? The man who takes care of your mother?"

CHAPTER TWENTY-FOUR

NOAH RUBBED HIS hands up and down Reese's arms in an effort to keep her warm. The first towel Brynn had given her to dry off had been soaked by the time she'd wiped the water off her exposed skin. The one she currently had around her shoulders was now damp from collecting the moisture from her clothes. It didn't help that the central air of the bar was cooling the place even more now that the majority of the town had been told to vacate the premises.

"I'm so sorry, Reese," Cassie barely managed to whisper through the hoarseness she'd acquired from crying for the last hour. "I tried to explain everything to you at the diner earlier this evening, but I just couldn't bring myself to tell you what I'd done."

"You hired Darcy to attack Reese, Cassie." Noah wasn't in the forgiving frame of mind. Sheriff Percy needed to put this woman in cuffs and take her away before Noah decided to do it for him. "Reese was physically assaulted and had to be treated by paramedics. What if she'd suffered a concussion or worse? Did you ever think of that?"

"Noah, d-don't." Reese was having some minor trouble keeping her teeth from chattering, but Noah couldn't take her home quite yet. The sheriff was still trying to piece together what was related to the actual events compared to the body they'd discovered in his home. "Cassie, I still d-don't understand why you tried to s-scare me away."

"You came to town asking all these questions about Emma. I didn't think anything of it until I heard that you were really trying to find out what happened to Sophia." Cassie wiped away her tears with a couple of white napkins she'd taken from one of the tables. "It was only a matter of time before you figured out that she snuck out of camp to talk to my mom. I didn't want those damned nude photographs from so many years ago making my mother's life impossible back here in our hometown, especially when it was so hard to make them disappear in the first place."

"And this is when you asked Darcy to attack Ms. Woodward?"

Sheriff Percy shook his head in disappointment. Noah was also in disbelief that one of their own could resort to such heinous measures.

"You don't have to stay here for this," Noah whispered, deciding it might be better take Reese home while the sheriff sorted this out.

"Yes, I do." Reese pasted a smile on her face as Brynn brought her yet another towel, though this time it was accompanied by a blanket. "Thank you so much."

"It's no problem," Brynn said with a side-eye toward Cassie in disgust. "You just let me know if you need anything else."

"Darcy didn't mean to hurt you, Reese." Cassie pressed the back of her hand to her trembling lips, trying to maintain her composure. "He only meant to scare you. We just wanted you to leave town, Reese. That's all. He was horrified when he'd heard just how badly you'd been injured when pushed you against the tiled wall. He didn't mean to do it so hard.

Reese. And then he was afraid you'd recognize him. He's always in and out of the diner with my mom."

"He did hurt me, Cassie." Reese handed Noah the damp towel and then wrapped herself in the warmth of the soft blanket. A little color was coming back into her cheeks, but that might have had to do with the shot of whiskey Rose had brought over from the bar. "And everything you've done has made me question the good intentions of everyone I've met in Blyth Lake. They didn't deserve my suspicion, and what you've done could very well have kept others from telling me about Sophia. They believed it was too dangerous to talk to me."

"Don't you understand," Cassie practically begged, leaning forward with the napkins wadded up inside her fingers, "what those photographs would have done to my mother, the diner, and even me had they been rediscovered? Those pictures weren't just nude photographs, Reese. They were pornography in the worst way, because my mother made a mistake that she shouldn't have to suffer for over and over. These people would have crucified her. They aren't going to tolerate her past mistakes."

"You didn't give the people of this town a chance to prove you otherwise, Cassie," Noah answered in a hardened tone, not even attempting to hide his disgust. "You and Darcy went too far with this cover-up over something you thought might hurt your business. It had nothing to do with your mom's reputation."

"I'm inclined to agree with Noah," Sheriff Percy said in disappointment as he nodded toward one of the younger deputies who had stayed behind while Deputy Foster had accompanied Darcy to the hospital. The deputy stepped forward. "It also has me wondering if it wasn't Darcy out in those woods that night when Deputy Wallace was killed. Did Wallace recognize Darcy? Was he using the shortcut to walk toward Ms. Woodward's residence and then panicked when he saw my deputy standing guard out at the old Yoder place?"

"You think—" Cassie cheeks had been rather flushed from all the tears she'd cried this evening, but every bit of color drained from her face at the sheriff's implication. "No. No, no, no. Darcy didn't kill Deputy Wallace, Sheriff. He didn't. After things started getting out of hand is when Darcy tried to warn Reese away. After that, he stayed far away from her, because he feared she would recognize him. He wasn't near her house that night, Sheriff. I promise you."

"I guess we'll have to find that out on our own now, won't we?" Sheriff Percy gestured toward the deputy to take Cassie into custody. "You took matters into your own hands and created a hell of a mess here. You're just as guilty as Darcy, Cassie. You're under arrest for—"

"Wait." Reese held up her hand as if she could stop what was about to happen. "This is getting—"

"Cassie?"

All eyes turned toward the entrance of the bar. Annie Osburn stood there in all her glory using a cane to help her slowly advance toward her daughter.

"Mama?" Cassie's eyes filled with even more tears as she practically broke down in the chair. "I'm so sorry. You weren't ever supposed to—"

"I wasn't supposed to know that you hired Darcy to scare off this poor woman?" Annie Osburn wasn't one to take any prisoners. She was a woman in her own right, but she was also a mother whose every decision had been based on ensuring her daughter was raised properly. "I figured something was up between the two of you with all those secret conversations in the kitchen. I could hear you two whispering like you were a couple of teenagers. I might be old, Cassandra Mae, but I'm not deaf. But to do something so awful?"

Noah had been standing over Reese this entire time, but he pulled up a chair so that he could sit next to her. What he had to say, no one else needed to hear. Cassie was too busy trying to condone her choices and actions, so he used this time to see what was on Reese's mind.

"What were you going to say before Annie walked in the door?" Noah asked softly, tucking some damp strands of hair behind her ear. It irritated him that she was still shivering on and off, when he could have her home on the couch with dry clothes. "Cassie and Darcy committed a crime, sweetheart. That can't go unanswered."

"Do you really believe that they had anything to do with the body we found?" Reese grabbed Noah's hands and held them close, leaning into him for support. She wasn't looking for him to agree with her, because it appeared she'd already made up her mind. He'd have to change it, because the bulky bandages on her hands reminded him of how severe her injuries could have been had she not fought as hard as she had. "I'm positive that when Sheriff Percy or Detective Kendrick investigate Darcy, they will find that he didn't kill Deputy Wallace. All this is doing is muddying the water, and potentially allowing whoever was responsible for Emma's death to remain free."

"Do you forget what took place an hour ago?" Noah reminded Reese, needing her to see what she was suggesting wasn't the wisest call to make right this moment. "Darcy was going to physically attack you *again*. He—"

"But he didn't." Reese rubbed her forehead as she attempted to conjure up exactly what had taken place out in that alleyway. Her action drew his attention to her scar. "I think he was trying to apologize, just as Cassie suggested to us earlier. I didn't give him the chance."

"Do you want this happening to someone else? What happens when a reporter gets wind that Anastasia Pearl Osburn lives out in an old farmhouse to the east of town? Is Cassie going to take matters into her own hands again? Is Darcy going to follow along for a few hundred bucks?"

"I think we need to let the sheriff do his job here, but I'm not going to press charges." Reese surprised him by softly resting her bandaged palm on his cheek in a subtle plea that he wasn't sure he could accommodate. "Please understand my position. They made a mistake. It was a colossal one, I'll give them that, but it was an emotional mistake all the same."

Noah shook his head in disbelief that she could just let this go, although he wasn't certain the law would allow this to go unpunished. Simple assault was a Class A misdemeanor. She might not have any sway over the sentencing that would be handed down over this type of crime, but it was something they could discuss tomorrow.

Right now, he wanted to take her home.

There were many things on his mind, and quite a lot he wanted to say to Reese.

This wasn't the time or place.

The entrance to the Cavern opened once more, revealing Detective Kendrick. Noah breathed a sigh of relief. The sheriff might be handling this situation in the proper manner, but it was good to have someone on the outside conduct a fair investigation without emotion coming into play. Towns like these were known to sweep their dirt under the rug a time or two.

"Detective, I'm glad you were able to come," Noah said as he offered his hand. The firm handshake lasted a little too long, alerting him to the fact that something was wrong. What else could have happened this evening? "Reese, would you please give me a moment?"

Reese didn't have time to answer as Annie took his vacant

seat. She was rather quick for an old-timer, but it didn't take a genius to figure out that she was apologizing for what her daughter had done.

"First, I don't want you to worry about Darcy Tillman or Cassie Osburn. I'll be taking over the investigation shortly." Detective Kendrick didn't stop walking until he'd led Noah across the room where no one could hear what he had to say next. His grim expression had Noah steeling himself for the news about to be delivered. "The DNA results came back from the lab."

"I think we all knew it was Emma Irwin," Noah guessed with a shake of his head. It wasn't like the entire town hadn't known who had been killed and hidden inside that wall all those years ago, but it was still hard to swallow that evil of this kind could exist among the residents of this town. With that said, he never would have guessed that Cassie and Darcy would have attacked an innocent woman all because she'd asked a few questions about the past. "Have you told her family?"

"Noah, it wasn't Emma."

Detective Kendrick allowed his words to penetrate, but even then, Noah had a difficult time accepting them as the truth.

"I saw what hair was still there," Noah said rather cautiously as a sinking awareness in the pit of his stomach took up residence. "It was the same length, the same color…"

It could have been the look on the detective's face, or it could have been a simple deduction of reasoning, but Noah was already denying where his thoughts had taken him.

"No." Noah flat out denied what Kendrick was about to confirm. "No, that's not possible. Anderson installed that drywall before—"

"Pete Anderson didn't construct that additional room until a year after Emma went missing. They weren't even living there until more than a year after renovations began." Detective Kendrick laid a compassionate gaze on Reese when all Noah wanted to do was turn back time. This news was going to devastate her. "I wanted you to know first, so you can be there for her."

"How conclusive are the results?"

There could have been a mistake at the lab. Noah was grasping at straws, but he didn't want to pile onto the load Reese was already under tonight.

"Noah, the body you and Ms. Woodward discovered behind that drywall was Sophia Morton. The lab ran the whole series of tests twice," Detective Kendrick confirmed before gesturing toward Reese. "I'm sorry to be the bearer of bad news, but I promise you I will do everything in my power to catch the son of a bitch who put her in there."

CHAPTER TWENTY-FIVE

Three weeks later...

"**G**OOD MORNING."

Reese smiled tenderly at the rich tone of Noah's voice first thing in the morning. She patted the cushioned seat next to her on the porch swing, waiting for him to join her. Once his warm body was next to hers, she snuggled in underneath his arm and curled her legs up beneath her.

"Good morning." Reese raised her face for her morning kiss. This had become somewhat of a ritual, though there were times he woke her with a kiss in bed. "Sleep well?"

"No," Noah chuckled, resting his chin on top of her head as they both stared out over the front yard. They were still staying in the rental house. In another day or two, Noah would be able to move into his new home. "Someone kept me up way past my normal bedtime."

"Hmmm," Reese hummed in remembrance, her body tingling all over at just the mention of their lovemaking. "From my standpoint, it was well worth the lack of sleep."

A rather plump squirrel darted from behind one of the trees, and it wasn't long before his playmate joined him in a game of tag. It was silly really, but Reese wondered how long they'd been together. From birth? Or had they forged a friendship recently, and this was their way of getting to know one another?

"A kiss for your thoughts." Noah had brought with him a

cup of coffee, knowing she'd already have one in hand. Hers was currently sitting on top of the railing, while he held his in his left hand. "And maybe a refill on that coffee of yours."

"I want to stay."

Reese held herself still as she waited for Noah's response. She had to force herself to breathe when he didn't reply right away.

The devastating news that the body found within the walls of his first home had actually been Sophia had been crushing to hear that night. Reese had already suffered from numerous scratches and scrapes, having warded off who she thought at the time to be a killer. She'd grieved for years over her cousin's disappearance. She certainly hadn't been expecting such a blow after all this time.

Darcy Tillman's juvenile acts were nothing compared to the horrific ones done to Sophia, Deputy Wallace, and possibly Emma.

Reese had driven to Heartland that night with Detective Kendrick to deliver the news to her family. It had been the single worst thing she'd ever done in her life, but she hadn't been alone.

Noah had been by her side every minute since then, taking care of her, supporting her, and being there to hold her at night when the grief returned from all those years ago.

Sophia's body had been released to her family, and she'd been laid to rest next to her father. Whatever problems they may have had before were meaningless in the face of death. They were now together, both of them looking over the rest of the family.

Reese had come back to Blyth Lake with Noah for several reasons, though the main one being she'd found something here she wasn't ready to let go. She still wasn't.

"I came to Blyth Lake searching for answers," Reese shared, her heart skipping a beat as she filled the silence. She drew circles on the rough material of his jeans to keep herself from demanding he say something, but it might be better this way. He could finally hear what she'd been wanting to say for days. "I came in search of family, and in a way, I truly believe Sophia led me here…to you."

Noah inhaled deeply, as if he were getting ready to address her declaration. She thought she was ready to hear his response, but she was downright terrified that she might be wrong.

"Don't!" Reese shifted so that she could gaze into his blue eyes that had always met hers across a room when she needed reassurance. It was uncanny how he'd known she needed something to ground her when emotions had become too overwhelming. "I need you to know that me wanting to stay here has nothing to do with Sophia. My choice has nothing to do with the investigation. I don't know what the future holds, but I know that walking away is wrong. Walking away from *you* is wrong."

Reese took his coffee and set his mug next to hers, balancing herself on the porch swing as she once again faced him for his inevitable answer. She only had one more thing to say as she lifted her arms and crossed them over her chest to signify where here words were coming from.

This was it.

She was baring her soul to the one man who had the ability to destroy it.

"I've fallen for you, Noah Kendall."

THERE HAD BEEN numerous times in Noah's life where he'd experienced a soul-lifting feeling of relief. There had been the time his unit had been rescued after being pinned down by the enemy for a half an hour—they hadn't lost a single Marine that day, but the minutes had seemed like hours. There was getting the phone call that his father had come through his heart surgery with flying colors. There had even been the moment he'd signed his DD-214, reality sinking in that he was returning home alive, unlike some of his fellow servicemen and women who would never get that opportunity.

And then there was this one singular moment.

Today was the day Reese had been scheduled to return to Heartland for a week before heading back to Springfield to pick up where her life had left off at the beginning of this summer. It was surreal to think that she would no longer be lying next to him in bed, helping him renovate his home, laughing with him over old stories told by his father, or simply being by his side.

He'd struggled to find the words to explain how much she'd come to mean to him since his return to Blyth Lake. The speech he'd agonized over saying this morning evaporated into the warm morning air upon her declaration.

She wanted to stay.

She'd fallen for him.

Reese sat in front of him with sheer honesty shining from her brown eyes filled with unshed tears. She grew more and more beautiful with each passing day, and he had no doubt that he would feel the same way in fifty years as he did this moment.

Mary Kendall had been right about love. Once it was found, there was no denying it.

"You know, I had an entire speech planned out, with airtight reasons why you couldn't leave." Noah took her by the wrists and pulled her onto his lap, easing his ache to hold her. He captured her lips and kissed her as passionately as he had the first time in her kitchen. They were both out of breath by the time they were done. He rested his forehead against hers, staring into her caramel gaze. "But only one reason matters, Reese Woodward, and that is I love you."

"It took you long enough," Reese laughed while at the same time holding back a sob of happiness. "I can't even wrap my head around what needs to be done yet, but—"

"We've got this." Noah gently brushed her hair away from her eyes, still feeding this aching need inside of him to touch her. "You and me, sweetheart. We've handled everything thrown our way. We're stronger together, and we've proven that time and again."

Noah lifted Reese into his arms, leaving behind the two cups of coffee in favor of the bedroom. Soon, similar mugs would be on a different porch…their porch. He'd been given a home by his mother and father, and now he had a woman by his side to rebuild the foundation.

They had exposed an unbelievable nightmare in this town created by an evil that shouldn't be able to exist among these good people.

They had also unlocked a love that could conquer anything thrown in its way, including fear. The tables had turned. It was evil that feared the light of day now. They would strive to push the perpetrator responsible for killing Sophia out into the light, even if it took every ounce of energy that the Kendalls could muster.

~ The End ~

Thank you for joining me in the beginning of the Kendall family's journey in unraveling a mystery that has surrounded Blyth Lake for twelve long years. You're not going to want to miss the continuation into Lance Kendall's story with Unlocking Secrets…

HERE

www.kennedylayne.com/keys-to-love-book-two-mdash-unlocking-secrets.html

A grim discovery in Lance Kendall's home proved one thing—the residents of Blyth Lake had a serial killer in their midst. Now Lance had unintentionally put a target on his back. Worst yet, he's made the only woman he ever loved known to a murderer.

A trip down memory lane with the man who'd broken Brynn Mercer's heart wasn't the smartest thing she'd ever done in her life, but their reunion was a slow burn of temptation that she couldn't ignore.

Together, they will only have one chance to correct the past. Will the hidden secrets he uncovered threaten their love or solidify it for a future that has always been out of their reach?

Books by Kennedy Layne

Keys to Love Series

Unlocking Fear (Keys to Love, Book One)
Unlocking Secrets (Keys to Love, Book Two)
Unlocking Lies (Keys to Love, Book Three)
Unlocking Shadows (Keys to Love, Book Four)
Unlocking Darkness (Keys to Love, Book Five)

Surviving Ashes Series

Essential Beginnings (Surviving Ashes, Book One)
Hidden Ashes (Surviving Ashes, Book Two)
Buried Flames (Surviving Ashes, Book Three)
Endless Flames (Surviving Ashes, Book Four)
Rising Flames (Surviving Ashes, Book Five)

CSA Case Files Series

Captured Innocence (CSA Case Files 1)
Sinful Resurrection (CSA Case Files 2)
Renewed Faith (CSA Case Files 3)
Campaign of Desire (CSA Case Files 4)
Internal Temptation (CSA Case Files 5)
Radiant Surrender (CSA Case Files 6)
Redeem My Heart (CSA Case Files 7)

About the Author

First and foremost, I love life. I love that I'm a wife, mother, daughter, sister… and a writer.

I am one of the lucky women in this world who gets to do what makes them happy. As long as I have a cup of coffee (maybe two or three) and my laptop, the stories evolve themselves and I try to do them justice. I draw my inspiration from a retired Marine Master Sergeant that swept me off of my feet and has drawn me into a world that fulfills all of my deepest and darkest desires. Erotic romance, military men, intrigue, with a little bit of kinky chili pepper (his recipe), fill my head and there is nothing more satisfying than making the hero and heroine fulfill their destinies.

Thank you for having joined me on their journeys…

Email:

kennedylayneauthor@gmail.com

Facebook:

facebook.com/kennedy.layne.94

Twitter:

twitter.com/KennedyL_Author

Website:

www.kennedylayne.com

Newsletter:

www.kennedylayne.com/newsletter.html